To Fudge or Not to Fudge

"*To Fudge or Not to Fudge* is a superbly crafted, classic, culinary cozy mystery. If you enjoy them as much as I do, you are in for a real treat."
—**Examiner.com** (5 stars)

"We LOVED it! This mystery is a vacation between the pages of a book. If you've never been to Mackinac Island, you will long to visit, and if you have, the story will help you to recall all of your wonderful memories."
—*Melissa's Mochas, Mysteries and Meows*

"A five-star delicious mystery that has great characters, a good plot, and a surprise ending. If you like a good mystery with more than one suspect and a surprise ending, then rush out to get this book and read it, but be sure you have the time, since once you start, you won't want to put it down."
—**Mystery Reading Nook**

"A charming and funny culinary mystery that parodies reality-show competitions and is led by a sweet heroine, eccentric but likable characters, and a skillfully crafted plot that speeds toward an unpredictable conclusion. Allie stands out as a likable and engaging character. Delectable fudge recipes are interspersed throughout the novel."
—*Kings River Life*

All Fudged Up

A MIDSUMMER
NIGHT'S FUDGE

Nancy Coco

Kensington Publishing Corp.
www.kensingtonbooks.com

KENSINGTON BOOKS are published by

Kensington Publishing Corp.
119 West 40th Street
New York, NY 10018

All Kensington titles, imprints, and distributed lines are available at special quantity discounts for bulk purchases for sales promotion, premiums, fund-raising, educational, or institutional use.

Special book excerpts or customized printings can also be created to fit specific needs. For details, write or phone the office of the Kensington Sales Manager: Attn.: Sales Department. Kensington Publishing Corp., 119 West 40th Street, New York, NY 10018. Phone: 1-800-221-2647.

The K and Teapot logo is a trademark of Kensington Publishing Corp.

First Printing: June 2022
ISBN: 978-1-4967-3553-9

ISBN: 978-1-4967-3554-6 (ebook)

10 9 8 7 6 5 4 3 2 1

Printed in the United States of America

This book is dedicated to my dad, Thaddeus J. Kozicki Jr., who was always the smartest man in the room. God took you too soon. You are loved and missed and always in our hearts.

Chapter 1

I'd much rather make fudge and celebrate festivals with my friends than find murder victims. But finding victims seems to be my luck these days. Of course, murder victims were the last thing on my mind as we celebrated the very first Midsummer Night's Festival. The July festival celebrated summer on the island and opened with an outdoor masquerade ball, bonfire on the beach, and crowning of the Midsummer Night's queen.

"Mrs. Higer really outdid herself with this ball," I said as Jenn and I exited the dance floor. Jenn was my best friend and sometimes partner in sleuthing. Recently married, Jenn was gorgeously slim, wearing a black jumpsuit and large blue butterfly wings. Her wide brown eyes were half hidden behind a black eye mask made of lace.

"I think Mayor Boatman is trying to take some credit

for the event," Jenn said and pointed to where the mayor stood beside Winona Higer as people congratulated her. The mayor wore a long gown and a Marie Antoinette wig. She had a beauty patch on her cheek and a silver eye mask. There was no mistaking Mayor Boatman, even in costume. Winona also stood out in a lovely white gown with rainbow hair and a unicorn headdress.

It was Jenn's idea to have a masquerade ball and we loved how people went all in with fairy costumes and general midsummer fun. We set up the festivities on the beach with the big bonfire nearby, seating for anyone who wanted it, and then the dance area where people moved energetically. The dance floor itself was a ten-by-ten-foot deck that rested on the sandy beach, while a live band played. There were cash bars on either side of the event area and the large bonfire to the left, where people sat in grouped lawn chairs while others put out picnic blankets and coolers.

There was a long buffet table and Porter's meats had roasted a pig. Little kids dressed as fairies and unicorns ran through the sand, laughing and squealing as they chased each other. Brave souls swam in the cool water of Lake Michigan, running out to dry off by the fire and jumping back into the water.

I was not swimming. Not that I didn't like to swim, but I had recently gotten a cast off my arm and was happy to dress fancy for the ball in a floaty, green gown with a kerchief hem and huge fairy wings. My bichon-poo pup, Mal, was in the mix dressed as a dragon. She loved festivals and people. Thankfully, my boyfriend Rex Manning didn't mind watching her while I danced.

We returned to our spot where Rex and Jenn's new

husband, Shane Carpenter, sat drinking beer and watching the flames grow and pop as people added fuel to the bonfire.

Mal barked and jumped up on me and I picked her up, giving her a quick squeeze as she licked my face.

"Hurry up and take a seat," Shane said. "They're about to pick the queen and her court."

I sat down in a lawn chair next to Rex. My boyfriend was a police officer and with his shaved head and gorgeous blue eyes, he had that action-hero look to him. Shane, on the other hand, was lanky with thick glasses and caramel-colored hair. Both of the men had indulged us by wearing black T-shirts, jeans, and eye masks. After all, the event was a masquerade.

"Ladies and gentlemen, your attention please," Winona said, her voice loud through the microphone in her hand. We all turned to look at the main stage. Five young ladies stood on the stage in long, flowing gowns complete with fairy wings and pointed ears. "As you know, these girls have been competing for the last three days in various portions of the contest: talent, health, and interview. Now the scores have been calculated and are currently being verified by the local accountants of Bradford Accounting. Mr. Bradford, could you please bring up the results."

Everyone clapped as the accountant in black-tie attire and a black mask walked up and handed her an envelope. He then motioned for her to bend down and whispered in her ear.

"I see," Winona said. "Thank you. Tonight, ladies and gentlemen, you see five girls in front of you, but due to a disqualification, there will only be four places awarded for the queen and her court. Your queen will receive a five-hundred-dollar scholarship to the school of her choice and she and her court will ride in the queen's float in tomorrow's parade."

As the crowd clapped, the girls looked at each other, puzzled. Who was disqualified?

"The third runner-up is . . . Alicia Newhouse." Everyone clapped as the lovely blonde received flowers and a sash. "The second runner-up is . . . Lakesha Smith." The beautiful girl with the chocolate skin stepped up and received her sash. "There are three girls left," Winona said. "And only one winner. The first runner-up is . . . Madison Oustand." Everyone clapped as the curvy brunette received her flowers and sash and the two remaining girls stood together and held hands.

"Two girls stand before us. Each one lovely. Each one receiving high marks for community service, health, and interview. Unfortunately, only one is the queen. And the winner is . . . Julie Vanderbilt!" Everyone clapped as the tall brunette clasped her hands over her mouth and cried. "Unfortunately, that means Natasha Alpine has been disqualified. You may leave the stage."

"There must be some kind of mistake," Natasha said. "I'm a queen. Why would I be disqualified?"

"We've been made aware of an error in your community service hours," Winona said. "Now let's crown our queen." She shooed Natasha off the stage and took the tiara out of the hands of her assistant, Michelle Bell, and pinned it into Julie's hair. Then placed a sash around her dress and handed her roses. With a flourish, Winona waved the crowd to clap over their queen. But Natasha had not left the stage, so Winona attempted to encourage her out of the way. But Natasha continued to argue that the crown was hers, until Bill Blachek grabbed her by the waist and pulled her off the stage.

"Now it's time for the fireworks," Winona said into the microphone.

"Seems like there were a lot of fireworks already," Jenn said with a laugh.

We turned to the sky as the fireworks shot up over the straits of Mackinac and exploded into the air with loud booms. Mal was not a fan and jumped into my lap. I wrapped her tightly in a blanket, but she still shivered.

"I'm going to run Mal home," I said. "I'll be right back."

"Do you want me to come with you?" Rex asked.

"No, I'll be fine."

I lived at the top of the Historic McMurphy Hotel and Fudge Shop. It was on Main Street just a few blocks from the beach. Hugging Mal as fireworks exploded and people oohed and aahed, I scurried through the crowd. As I passed by, I noticed that Winona was busy arguing with Natasha and what appeared to be her mother and her grandmother about the disqualification. I shook my head and headed up from the beach and onto the sidewalk, past the school and onto Main.

The festival drew most of the people from the island, so Main Street was unusually quiet. I unbundled Mal and let her walk/run back to the McMurphy with me. Hurrying down the alley around the back, I saw that Mal was better, since we were no longer right in front of the fireworks. Poor pup, I hadn't realized how terrible fireworks were for pets. Thankfully, I had a comfort shirt for her, so I took her upstairs, put her in her shirt, gave her a chew bone, checked on my kitty, Mella, and then locked the door. The fireworks were slowing down as I left Main Street and walked the footpath to the beach.

Then, just as the last fireworks exploded, I saw something in the water. Glancing around, I didn't see anyone nearby, so I hurried to the water's edge.

It was a woman in a unicorn costume. The white dress with rainbow hair flowed in and out with the waves.

I dove into the water and turned her so that her face was out of the water and dragged her to shore, as I was taught in my high school lifeguard class. I got maybe a yard onto dry sand when I heard someone approach.

"Allie, are you okay?" It was Mrs. Tunisian. She was a dear friend and one of a handful of senior citizens retired on the island. She was dressed as a dragonfly with her hair in a mohawk and a headband with twin antennae.

"I'm fine," I said, "but she isn't. She was in the water." I set down the woman and gasped as I saw it was Winona. I went to my knees to push water from her lungs when I noticed a dark, round hole in the center of her forehead.

I grabbed my phone and turned on the flashlight.

"Oh, that's not good," Mrs. Tunisian said.

Indeed, it was not. Winona had been shot right between the eyes. I don't think there was anything I could do to save her life.

"Run back to the bonfire and get Rex," I ordered Mrs. Tunisian. Then I dialed 911.

"This is 911, what is your emergency?" Charlene, the operator asked.

"Hi, Charlene," I said, my voice breathless.

"Oh, my goodness, Allie, who's dead?" It seemed to be a growing theme between me and Charlene.

"It's Mrs. Higer," I said. "She's been shot."

"Is she alive?"

"No, I don't think so," I said. "I found her in the water and when I pulled her out, I saw that she had a bullet hole in the center of her forehead."

"Where are you?"

"I'm at the beach, just at the bottom of the path from Main Street."

"I've got police arriving soon," Charlene said. "Are you okay? Did you see the shooter?"

"No," I said, looking around. "I didn't see the shooter, but her body is still warm. It had to have happened not too long ago."

"Does she have a heartbeat?"

I placed my fingers on the side of her neck. "No," I said. "She's definitely dead."

In the distance, I heard the sirens from the ambulance coming my way. Mackinac Island had banned motor vehicles nearly a century ago. Which meant most people got around by bicycle or horse and carriage. I liked to walk everywhere. But when it came to safety, we had a modern fire truck and a modern ambulance. They were the only vehicles allowed on the island.

Rex and Mrs. Tunisian came running up, followed by Jenn and Shane.

"Allie, what happened? You're wet!" Jenn said.

"I was coming back down the path when I saw someone in the water. She was face down, so I swam out to get her and bring her in," I said

"That's when we saw the bullet hole in her forehead," Carol Tunisian said to Rex, who squatted down next to the body. "That's when I went to get you."

"Did anyone hear a shot?" I asked.

"The fireworks must have covered up the sound," Rex said.

Two bikes approached. It was Officer Lasko and Officer Brown.

Rex waved them down.

"It's Winona," I said and pointed toward the body. "Someone shot her in the head."

"Were you here when she was found?" Officer Charles Brown asked Rex. Charles was a handsome man with a strong chin and short brown hair.

"No," Rex said. "Allie found her in the water."

"I went and got Rex," Carol repeated. A crowd had begun to form behind Jenn.

"I'm going to go get my kit," Shane said. He was our local crime scene investigator.

"How did you find her?" Officer Megan Lasko asked. She pulled a notebook out of her pocket to take my statement.

I went over what happened. I knew from experience that I would be asked the same questions over and over to ensure I didn't change my story or to help me remember something I might have forgotten.

"Did you see anyone else?" Officer Lasko asked.

"No." I shook my head. "The fireworks must have covered the sound of the gunshot."

"What was she doing way over here?" Megan mused.

"I don't know," I said. "I found her in the water, so she could have drifted over here."

"Did you see her at the bonfire?"

"I did."

"Did you see her leave?" Megan asked.

"No," I said. "Last I saw her, she was talking to Natasha Alpine and her family."

The ambulance arrived and George Marron stepped out. He was dressed in a blue EMT's outfit, his hair pulled back into a long, single braid. His cheekbones were high and slashed across his thin face. His copper-colored skin shone in the light from my phone.

"Hello, Allie," he said.

"Hi, George," I greeted him.

"What do we have?"

"Winona, shot in the middle of her forehead," I said. "I don't think she needs you. You'd better call the coroner."

"Is Shane on duty?"

"He went home to get his kit," I said.

Jenn came over with a beach towel for me. I hadn't seen her leave, but there was a lot going on and it was dark. "Here," she said. "You're shivering."

I huddled into the warmth of the beach towel.

"I'll tape off the crime scene," Megan said. "The crowds are growing, and we don't need them trampling evidence."

Jenn hugged me. "Are you okay?"

"Yes," I said, hugging her back. "How did she get in the water?"

"Did you see anyone nearby when you found her?" Rex asked as he left the body to the officers on duty.

"No." I shook my head. "I didn't hear anything either. I think the shot was covered by the fireworks."

"Last I saw her, she was talking to the Alpines," Jenn said. "The conversation looked heated."

"I know," I said. "That's when I saw her."

"We're going to have to interview the people at the party and see if anyone saw her leave," Rex said.

"Well, then you'd better hurry, because people are leaving." I pointed toward a couple of people walking up the trail toward Main Street.

"I'm sure that anyone with information will come forward," Rex said with confidence. He turned to give me a glimpse of the crowd forming outside the tape lines. "It looks like everyone showed up for this crime scene."

"Maybe even the killer," Carol said.

If only things were ever that easy.

Fudgy Bottom Boozy Raspberry Swirl Cheesecake

This cheesecake has a brownie bottom and vodka-soaked raspberries pureed and swirled into it.

Ingredients:
For bottom:
12 tablespoons unsalted butter, melted
1¾ cups granulated sugar
1⅓ cups unsweetened cocoa powder
¼ teaspoon salt
3 large eggs
1 teaspoon vanilla extract

For cheesecake:
6 ounces raspberries
¼ cup of vodka
32 ounces of cream cheese (room temperature)
1¾ cups sugar
dash of salt
1 tcaspoon vanilla
4 large eggs (room temperature)
boiling water

Directions:
Soak raspberries overnight in vodka. This pulls the juices out of the berries and adds a little flavor.

Melt butter in a sturdy saucepan. Stir in sugar, cocoa, and salt. Add eggs one at a time. Mix until combined.

Don't overmix or the eggs will lose their rise. Add vanilla and stir.

Cover the bottom of a ten-inch springform pan with parchment paper. Pour brownie mix into the pan. Bake at 350 degrees F for ten minutes. Remove from heat and let cool.

Place cream cheese in a sturdy, large bowl and beat for two minutes until light. Then slowly add the sugar a little at a time. Add salt and vanilla and mix. Add eggs one at a time and mix between adding until all are combined.

Strain berries and puree in a food processor. Or just use a fork and mash them. Then push through a small-holed sieve to pull out as many seeds as possible.

Next, pour cheesecake mixture over the brownie mixture. Dot the top with raspberry puree. Take a knife and swirl it through the raspberries into the cheesecake until pretty. Then put the filled ten-inch springform pan into a roaster and fill with boiling water until halfway up the sides of the pan.

Put the roaster pan and cheesecake into a 350 degrees F preheated oven. Bake for 60–70 minutes until the sides are set and the center wobbles slightly. Remove from oven and onto cooling rack. Wait thirty minutes until cool and place in refrigerator overnight until set. Remove springform sides and cut into generous wedges. Enjoy!

Chapter 2

I didn't see Rex the rest of the night as they worked through the crime scene and the witnesses. There was nothing for me to do but pace in my apartment, while Mal followed me back and forth. My biggest worry was there was someone out there with a gun and brave enough to shoot Winona during a fireworks display and push her body into the water.

Who could have done such a thing and why? The bonfire masquerade was a huge success and had raised nearly five thousand dollars for the parks. Winona had been the catalyst for the new festival and had done a lot of the planning and execution of the event.

I finally gave up pacing and went downstairs to make fudge. I usually got up early to make the fudge batches that filled the counter before the first ferries arrived at ten, filled with tourists. I was in the middle of making dark chocolate cherry, my personal favorite, when Rex knocked on the window. I rushed out of the fudge shop to open the front door of the McMurphy Hotel. The first streaks of dawn filled the sky and the sounds of birds singing followed him inside.

"Did you get any sleep?" I asked and I moved through the lobby toward the fudge shop. It was best to not leave candy alone too long.

"None." He followed me and ran a hand over his handsome face.

"There's fresh coffee at the coffee bar," I said with a nod in the direction of the bar. While the McMurphy was over a hundred years old, I'd remodeled and implemented a few new things the past year. One of them was secure door locks and security cameras. Another was a coffee bar in the far-right corner where guests could get a fresh cup of coffee every morning.

Wordlessly, Rex headed toward the bar and I checked the temperature of the candy. It was at the perfect stage. Time to grab some potholders and maneuver the large copper pot so that the fudge poured out on the buttered marble slab in the center of the room. The marble was cooled with a constant flow of cold water underneath and would absorb the heat from the fudge, ensuring that it came out smooth and silky.

I set to work scraping the pot, then set it down and changed to the long paddles to scrape and fold the fudge as it cooled.

The door to the fudge shop opened and Rex stepped in with two cups of coffee. "I fixed you one as well," he said and put the cup on the counter. The fudge shop was enclosed in glass walls in the front right of the lobby. It used to be open to all, but with pets living in the McMurphy,

I'd closed it off. "Wow," he said. "You got a lot done. Let me guess: You didn't sleep either."

"It's hard to sleep knowing there's a killer on the loose," I said as I went around the table folding the fudge. "Whoever did it was pretty brazen to shoot her in the middle of a crowd like that."

"Brazen, yes," he said and took a sip of his coffee. His gaze watched me as I poured cherries on top of the fudge and folded it in. "But still clever. No one saw a thing and all anyone heard was fireworks, so the killer either had a silencer or timed the shot perfectly with the fireworks."

Frowning, I moved to a shorter scraper and began to make the loaf of fudge. Folding fudge was a meditative action for me. If I wasn't giving a demonstration and telling my Papa Liam's favorite fudge stories to tourists, I was usually efficient and thoughtful. "Well then, it could have been anyone there."

"The only thing I have to go on is that the Alpines were quite upset about Natasha being disqualified. A lot of people saw them surrounding Winona and arguing until Mr. Blachek interrupted them and sent them to see the Bradford accountants about the results."

I finished the fudge by cutting it into neat one-pound slabs. "That doesn't seem like enough motivation to kill someone," I said. "Does it?"

"Beauty pageants can be very competitive," Rex said.

I glanced up at him to see if he was kidding. His expression was serious. I added the fudge to a tray and put the tray in the counter, then walked over and took my coffee from the countertop. "Thanks," I said and took a sip. "Competitive or not, I simply can't understand killing for it."

He reached over and tucked a wayward strand of my

hair under my baker's cap. "People have been known to kill each other over a carton of cigarettes."

"That's terrible," I said. "Still, it seems like the Alpines are respected members of the community. Natasha was last year's lilac queen. Why would they stoop to killing someone?"

"I'm scheduled to interview them this morning and find out," he said. "But I have a feeling they are all going to lawyer up."

"That's not a bad thing, is it?" I opened the fudge shop door and let him out and then myself.

"It depends," Rex said. "If they get a lawyer that doesn't want them to talk, then there's nothing I can do. If they simply tell me what they were doing during the murder, then I can rule them out."

"There are lawyers who say not to speak, no matter what," I commented as we moved through the lobby and up the four flights of stairs to the top floor and my apartment. "Can I make you some breakfast?"

"Eggs would be great," he said as I opened my door. Mal bounced up and greeted us with a wagging stump tail and happy bounces. Rex picked her up and gave her scritches behind the ears.

"Sounds good to me too." I took off my chef coat for later fudge making and hung it carefully by the door. Then I took off my hat and moved to my kitchen. The apartment was small and open; the living area compact and filled with a beautiful new couch, rug, and two chairs. Then there was a breakfast bar that had a composite countertop and divided the room from the living space to the kitchen space.

Rex put Mal down and took a seat on one of the barstools that faced the kitchen. "Frankly, this one has me worried. The Alpines don't really have a strong motive and no one else has popped out as a suspect."

I cracked eggs into my cast-iron frying pan and let them sizzle. Next, I popped seed-filled bread into the toaster. "Who else would have wanted Winona dead? She did a great job at the festival. Everyone was filled with compliments."

"Maybe it had nothing to do with the festival," he mused, then shook his head. "I'm tired and shouldn't really be discussing any of this with you." He glanced at me as I turned the eggs over easy and grabbed two plates. "You know that, right?"

"I know," I said and plated two eggs for each of us, then buttered the toast and added two slices to each plate. "I'm sorry that now you have to dig into Winona's life. What does her husband think of all this?"

"She's a widow," he said as he ate his eggs.

"Then her spouse isn't a possible suspect," I said and took my first bite of egg. It was rich and hot with just the right crisp of butter.

"Are you going to get some sleep when Frances gets in?" he asked, changing the subject with a worried look in his eye.

"I'll take a nap," I promised. "What about you?"

"I can go a while without sleep," he said. "I'm not handling hot sugar."

I sent him a smile. "I appreciate your concern for my well-being, but I'm a big girl. I'll be careful."

He reached out and took my hand and pulled it up to his lips and kissed it. "I know," he said. "I like that about you, you know. Your independence and your spunk."

"Is *spunk* a nice way to say that I have a mind of my own?"

"Maybe," he said with a smile and finished his eggs, toast, and his coffee. "Maybe it just means you have spunk." He kissed my cheek and put his dishes in the sink. "I've got to get back to the office and prep for my interviews."

I stood and put my plate in the sink and turned to give him a big hug. "Try to get a nap yourself. Okay?"

"I will," he said and kissed me quick and hard, patted Mal on the head, and went out the kitchen door and down the back steps to the alley below.

I sighed long and low. "Well, Mal, it looks like we have another murder to investigate."

Mal gave a short bark.

"But first I have to finish making fudge," I said. I grabbed my hat and chef's coat. "Want to come downstairs and wait for Frances?"

Arf!

Chapter 3

Frances, my general manager, usually arrived at eight in the morning. Today was no different. She unlocked the McMurphy and stepped inside. Mal jumped up from her doggie bed and ran, then slid the last few feet to bash into Frances's shins with a joyous bounce. Mal wasn't big on barking, but she showed her happiness with the bounce in her step and the wag of her stump tail.

I finished my last batch of fudge—this one was turtle fudge with caramel and nuts—and stepped out into the lobby. The McMurphy hotel lobby held the fudge shop in the upper right. The upper left held a fireplace and two couches for people to sit and enjoy a fire while using the free Wi-Fi. The lower left held the registration desk and keys. That was basically Frances's office and where Mal had a dog bed to curl up during the day when I was doing fudge demonstrations. The lower right held the coffee bar and more seating with winged-back chairs and a couch. The back of the lobby held two sweeping staircases with an old-fashioned elevator in the middle.

"Good morning," I said to Frances as I removed my baker's hat and my chef's coat.

"Done already this morning?" Frances said from her seat behind the registration desk. "You must have been up very early."

"Never went to bed," I said with a shake of my head. "Worried about Rex."

"If you are going to date the man, you are going to have to trust that he will keep himself safe," Frances said. She was an older woman, in her early seventies, who had just married for the second time herself. This time to my handyman, Douglas Devaney, who just arrived through the back door.

"I heard you found Winona Higer dead," Douglas said as he hung up his coat and came into the lobby. "That must have been quite a shock." Douglas was a year older than Frances, with a balding head and grumpy green eyes. He usually wore jeans and a dress shirt even though he was doing most of the handiwork for me.

"It was," I said. "I mean, I just saw her alive and well and trying to talk the Alpines down from their upset about Natasha's disqualification."

"Heard about that," Frances said. "The Alpines are a force to be reckoned with. I wouldn't have wanted to be the one to explain to them that she was disqualified."

"What for?" Douglas asked.

"Apparently her community service hours weren't correct," Frances said.

"And Winona didn't have anything to do with that," I said. "If anything, the Alpines should be mad at Natasha for cheating."

"I hardly doubt they were mad enough to kill," Frances said.

"Are you going to the parade this morning?" I asked. "The queen and her court will be on a float."

"I'll be here," Frances said. "You can go. I'm sure everyone will come out to see if the Alpines show up to support the queen even though Natasha wasn't in the court."

"You should go," Douglas said to me. "Take Mal out and get some fresh air. You look tired."

"Thanks," I said wryly and tried to look perky. "A girl loves to know when she looks bad."

Frances smacked Douglas's arm. "The girl didn't get any sleep," she said. "But that doesn't mean you should tell her that it shows."

Douglas shrugged. "I was just saying that fresh air might do her some good."

"I'll tell you what," I said with a smile. "The parade is at ten a.m. I'll go take a short nap. Will that make you two feel better?"

"It couldn't hurt," Douglas said with sincerity in his gaze.

"He means well," Frances agreed and patted my hand. "I've got the front desk. The maid service we hired will be in at nine to clean the rooms as people start to leave. The fudge shop is full."

"Okay, then," I said. "I'll be upstairs. Come on, Mal, let's go take a nap together."

*　*　*

Later that morning the air was that gentle warmth of summer. A cool breeze blew off the straits and the sky was bright blue. Crowds gathered as tourists, which the locals lovingly called *fudgies*, poured off the ferry boats and onto the main street. The parade started at eleven.

"I like mingling with the crowds, don't you?" Jenn asked. She had come in shortly after I laid down for a nap and started her day. She worked her event-planning business from the office on the fourth floor of the McMurphy.

"There's a big one today," I said. "Probably for the parade. Some of the queen's court came from Mackinaw City and St. Ignace to draw more people in."

"Well, the murder certainly hasn't caused people to stay home."

I settled into my lawn chair next to Jenn's, Mal on my lap, watching the crowd. We were across from the marina with a good view of Main Street. The parade was to come down the full length of Main, up Market Street, and end at the fort.

"Allie." Michelle Bell walked up to us. "We need a judge to replace Winona. Could you come up and judge?"

"Me?" I was surprised by the request.

"Yes," she said. "It would be good to have some young blood on the committee. Would you do it?"

"Go on, do it," Jenn said and pushed me up. "I'll take care of Mal."

I left my seat and followed Michelle up to the judges' station. The sound of the marching band could be heard in the distance and I glanced at my phone. It was eleven o'clock. Volunteers had cleared the streets and the parade came down the wide path. There were at least fifteen floats from local businesses, along with three bands. Mayor Boatman stood on a podium in the center of town with a mega-phone, announcing each entry as if she were a television commentator.

"What am I judging on?" I asked.

"Most original," Michelle said. "Most beautiful and best overall."

"Got it," I said as she handed me a pad of paper.

"Think of each float on a scale of one to ten for each category. Then we'll add our scores and present the prizes."

The festival committee was to have been the judges, but with Winona gone, it was me, Michelle, Carol Tunisian, and Patricia Ramsfeld. I would do my best to be impartial, but Frances and I had helped with the seniors' float. I knew how lovely it was and might be a little biased.

"There's the Grand Hotel's float," Carol said as a float passed by, filled with flowers and a replica of the Grand Hotel's famous front porch. "You should have a float next year, Allie."

"We don't have a porch," I said.

"Well, you'll think of something and the entry fee is for a good cause," Carol said.

I could see the wheels turning in her head as she planned out what my float should look like. Then came the float with the festival queen and her court. It was festooned with flowers and a throne where Julie Vanderbilt sat, holding a bouquet of roses and waving to the crowd. "She is a fantastic queen," I said.

"Not if you go by the looks Natasha Alpine is giving the float," Carol said and pointed to the young woman across the street from us. Natasha stood dressed in a black T-shirt and black shorts, her hair pulled up in a messy bun making her look even younger than she was. She did indeed glare at the float. I watched as she turned to her mother and said something before storming off toward the ferry docks.

"I wonder if Rex got any information out of the Alpines," I said. "He was supposed to question them this morning."

"Because we all saw them arguing with Winona," Carol said as she watched the next float go by. "They had to have known they would be questioned. I'm surprised they didn't stick around and talk to Rex last night. I swear half the island was still there well after they took poor Winona away."

"Rex said they called in a lawyer," I said.

"Why? They didn't do it, did they?"

I shrugged. "That's what some people do. We've done it a couple of times."

"True," Carol agreed as the last float went by, followed by the last marching band.

I marked my points and Michelle took the pads of paper from each of us to tally.

"Ladies," Michelle said. "It looks like we all agreed on our winners." She got up and handed the results to Mayor Boatman, who looked more professional today in her own bobbed hair and a smart summer suit.

"She better hurry with the announcement," I said. "The crowd is getting nervous."

"Ladies and gentlemen," Mayor Boatman said. "Please wait while I announce the grand champion float. One moment as I confer with the judges."

She came over and said, in a low tone, "Are you all sure of your choices?"

"We are," we all said at the same time.

"Good." The mayor went back to make her announcement.

"Why did she do that?" I asked. "Our winners were clear."

"Mayor Boatman likes to add suspense to her announcements," Michelle said.

"The winner of most original float goes to Old Tyme Photos," she said and the crowd clapped. "The most beautiful award goes to the Grand Hotel." Again, clapping. "And finally, the best overall float this year is . . ." She paused. "Doud's grocery store."

The crowd cheered as the owner of the store stepped forward to receive the giant ribbon and shake the mayor's hand.

"Well, another successful festival is done," I said.

"Oh no," Michelle said. "There's a lot left to do before we put the festival to bed. I was hoping you wouldn't mind helping, Allie."

"What kinds of things need doing?"

"We need to tally all the payments and audit the results, among other things. Will you do it?"

I wasn't sure why Michelle wanted me to be a part of the committee, but I was always looking for a way to be more involved in the community.

"Sure," I agreed and stood.

"Great, we have a meeting tomorrow to go over next steps. I'll email you the details," Michelle said and hugged the pads of paper we used. "Thank you again for volunteering."

"Any time," I said and left the judging dais. I searched the crowd for Jenn and Mal and found them walking toward me. "That was interesting."

"You looked so professional up there," Jenn teased me. "You should be a judge next year, too."

"That's the thing. Michelle asked me to take Winona's place on the committee to help close out all the festival vendors and such."

"Great!" Jenn said. "Wonderful experience for next year."

"As long as nobody gets killed," I muttered and walked through the crowd to the McMurphy.

Turtle Fudge

Ingredients:
14 ounces of soft caramel pieces
1 tablespoon of heavy whipping cream
3 cups of semisweet chocolate chips
1 14-ounce can of sweetened condensed milk
¼ teaspoon of salt
2 teaspoons of vanilla
1½ cups of chopped pecans

Directions:
In a microwave safe bowl, microwave on high, caramel pieces and heavy whipping cream—stir every thirty seconds until melted and smooth.

In a microwave safe bowl, combine chocolate chips and sweetened condensed milk. Microwave on high, stirring every thirty seconds until chocolate is nearly all melted. It will continue to melt after you take it out. Stir until smooth. Add salt and vanilla. Stir.

Line an 8x8-inch pan with parchment paper. Pour in half the chocolate fudge. Add half the nuts. Pour caramel on top. Add remaining nuts and cover with remaining fudge.

Cool for 2 hours until set. Cut into one-inch pieces. Makes 64. Enjoy!

Chapter 4

"The killer is most likely a man, right?" Jenn asked.
"Why would you say that?" I opened the front door to the McMurphy.

The fudge shop was bustling with people and the lobby filled with people who had checked out and waited for a ferry. I loved the energy summer guests brought to the McMurphy. It really made the old girl come alive.

"Because women aren't likely to use a gun," Jenn said. "That's what I heard, anyway."

"If she's mad enough she might," I said.

"Wow, it's busy in here," Jenn said and pointed to the fudge shop where Frances had a line three deep. "You need to get a new assistant in here, or at least a part-time salesperson."

I sighed. "You're right, the twins I hired to intern left. They found full-time jobs in Chicago and most of the kids on the island already have part-time jobs. I sure miss Sandy." Sandy Everheart had been my assistant last year, but had moved on to work in the kitchen of the Grander Hotel.

"I'll ask around and see if there isn't someone looking for part-time work."

I turned toward the fudge shop to help Frances when I spotted Rex in the back talking to Douglas. "I wonder what Rex is doing here?" Mal barked and I unhooked her from her leash so she could run up and greet Rex.

"What if he just misses you?" Jenn asked and grinned at me.

I tried to swat her arm, but she dodged me and went upstairs to the office. I helped Frances ring up the fudge buyers until the crowd thinned. "That was quite a run," I said.

"They came in after the parade," Frances said as we both left the fudge shop. Mal ran back and forth from me to Rex and Douglas, so I followed Mal over to where the two men talked.

"Hi, Rex, what's up?" I gave him a kiss on the cheek. He turned his head and gave me a quick kiss on my mouth. It surprised me. He usually didn't like public displays of affection while he was in his uniform.

"Rex was telling me that he might have a suspect in Winona's murder," Douglas said.

"Michelle Bell said she thought she saw someone talking with Winona," Rex said. "But I really would like more confirmation before I haul them in."

"I've got a Rotary Club meeting. I'll ask around to see if anyone saw anything," Douglas said.

"Are you here on official business?" I asked.

"I really came to see if you wanted to get some lunch,"

Rex said. "I've got about an hour and thought it would be great to spend it with you."

"Oh," I said and brushed a wayward hair from my face. "Sure, but the restaurants are sure to be packed since the parade just ended. Why don't we grab something from Doud's and bring it back? We could eat it on the rooftop deck."

"Sounds like a plan," Rex said.

"Do you want us to bring you back anything?" I asked Douglas.

"Ham and cheese on rye," he said. "Frances is fond of their soup. Bring some of that and a turkey and Swiss for her." He put his hand in his pocket to pull out his wallet.

"It's okay," I said and put my hand on his arm. "This one is on me."

"Thanks," he grumbled. "Rex, see you around." Douglas nodded his head and went toward Frances. I pulled out my phone.

"Who are you texting?" Rex asked.

"Jenn, to see if she wants us to bring her anything," I said. Jenn replied quickly. "And that's a no. She and Shane have a lunch date. I'm going to leave Mal here. Why don't we go out the back?"

"Sounds good," Rex said and opened the door for me.

I stepped out into the alley and smiled at him. My heart always did a soft pitter-pat at his gorgeous blue eyes ringed with black lashes and his square jaw.

He put his police cap on and glanced around as we stepped out.

"I'm glad you stopped by," I said as we walked the alley toward Doud's. "I understand the Alpines were less than helpful."

Rex shook his head. "Word travels fast in a small

town. Yes, they didn't have much to say and were completely alibied up. At least they each said they were with the other, so beyond that I have nothing more to keep them on."

I shook my head. "What about the person Michelle saw? Have you questioned them?"

"They're coming in this afternoon," he said. "But it doesn't mean they are the killer."

"It has to be someone everyone knows," I said. "Because no one, besides Michelle, has come forward about a killer. Which means what they saw was someone they expected to be on the beach that night."

"Who brings a gun to a bonfire anyway?" Rex asked.

"I also wondered that. If it were the Alpines, maybe they brought it for protection?"

"Protection from whom?"

"I don't know." I shrugged. "The riffraff? They're pretty hoity-toity. Maybe the jewelry Natasha was wearing was worth a fortune and Mrs. Alpine wanted to have a gun in case someone tried to steal it?"

"That rarely happens on the island. We had some tourists at the bonfire, but most people were locals."

"And locals don't steal if they are desperate?" I asked.

"Right" He looked thoughtful. "I don't know anyone so desperate that they would try to steal gems from Natasha. I mean, how would they get off the island if they did? Ferries didn't run until morning."

"I suppose you're right," I said as we approached the end of the alley. "Do you think the murder was premeditated?"

"Not sure," he said as we walked the sidewalk around the corner to the front of the grocery store. The crowds were still thick and spilled into the streets, mixing with carriages and working horse carts carrying luggage. He opened the door for me and we stepped inside. Doud's was the oldest grocery on the island, and with a prominent place on Main Street was always bustling. It was an old building with tin ceilings and tall shelves, but they had an up-to-date salad and soup bar and a grill in the back, along with stacks of boxed sandwiches for people who wanted a quick meal and didn't want to wait to be seated.

I grabbed a carry cart and headed straight for the salad bar. Rex picked one up as well and followed behind. "I'll get the soup and salad if you pick up the sandwiches."

"Sure thing," he said.

I watched him move efficiently about the store. I also noted how the women's gazes followed his broad back and narrow waist. He looked like an action hero and he was my action hero. What took me so long to understand that?

"I heard that the killer was Elias Sumner," a woman said behind me. "He was Winona's gardener and they got into a row that day over the way he was trimming her rosebushes."

I turned around to see Gracie Hammerstein talking to Mary Emry.

"Okay," Mary said as she stocked shelves.

"What, you don't think it's likely?" Gracie sounded offended. "Well, who do you think did it?"

Mary shrugged. "No telling. I didn't see anything."

"Well," Gracie continued. "Irene said she heard from Susan that the Alpines were questioned and let go. They got a good lawyer and there wasn't anything Rex could do to shake their story."

"It's just gossip," Rex whispered in my ear and I startled.

"Oh! I didn't know you had come over this way."

"I could tell," he said with a grin.

"You do know that sometimes gossip holds kernels of truth," I said to him.

"Most times it does not," he said and guided me toward the cash register. The whole encounter got me thinking. Mary Emry didn't talk much, but she worked nearly every day at Doud's. That meant she had access to a lot more gossip than I did. Maybe it was time to ask Mary more questions about what people were saying, but not when I was with Rex. He tended to frown on my amateur sleuthing.

Chapter 5

I started my last fudge demonstration of the day at 4 p.m. After making a batch of fudge, I had Frances help me pour the thick, hot fudge onto the cold marble table. Then I started with a long-handled spatula scraping and turning the fudge as it cooled. "They say fudge was first invented at Vassar, where women would make it in the dorms at night after curfew," I said. "They called it Vassar chocolate. But fudge has been produced on Mackinac Island since the 1880s. With the availability of inexpensive refined sugar, fudge became a popular candy because it was relatively easy to make. Mackinac Island has taken fudge to the next level with gourmet flavors and new twists." It was time to add the mixed-in ingredients. This fudge was dark chocolate mint, with mint chips and chocolate chips blended into the dark chocolate. I grabbed my small spatula and quickly flipped the candy, mixing in the chips and creating a long loaf of fudge. Then I cut the end off of the fudge and created small, taster pieces. I scooped them up and put them on a plate for Frances to hand out to the crowd. Lastly, I cut it into one-pound pieces and added it to a tray that fit into the fudge counter.

I rang up orders alongside Frances until the crowd dissipated. "I need to put up a sign for some help," I said as Frances and I walked out of the shop. "Do you know of anyone who wants part-time work?"

"I'll ask around," Frances said. "I still have ties to the high school. If you don't mind a younger person."

"I don't mind at all," I said. "Mostly it would be nice to free you up for check-ins and checkouts." We had a full house this week because Jenn had booked the Westminsters' wedding. The couple filled the McMurphy with friends and family. They intended to marry at St. Anne's and then have their reception on the rooftop deck. I knew Jenn would be up in the office, busy with all the last-minute details. "Do you need any help? If not, I'll change and go put an ad in the paper."

"Go right ahead," Frances said. "Most of the family has checked in already, so there's not that much to do."

I hurried upstairs and stripped out of my black pants and white shirt uniform and put on jeans and a T-shirt. Then I hooked up Mal to her leash and went out the back door. We met Mr. Beecher in the alleyway.

"Hello, Allie," he said. "Great evening, isn't it?"

Mr. Beecher came down the alley twice a day on his walks. He was an older man with a white beard and mustache, and he liked to wear waistcoats and suit jackets along with a hat. He reminded me of the snowman from the old *Rudolph the Red-Nosed Reindeer* stop-action show.

"Early evening," I said and glanced at my phone to see it was five o'clock. Mal did her business and then raced toward Mr. Beecher, who always had a treat in his pocket. "How are you? Did you see the parade?"

"Yes," he said. "Sheila and I enjoyed it. I agree with the judges, by the way. Nice job."

I felt my cheeks warm. "Thanks," I said. "I was called in at the last minute to replace Mrs. Higer. I really didn't know what to expect."

"Well, you did very well," he said. "It's too bad about Winona." He shook his head. "She was a good woman. Sheila loved her."

Shelia was Mr. Beecher's girlfriend and a lover of cats. "I think it's the saddest thing ever," I admitted.

"I understand you found Winona shortly after she was killed," he said.

"I did. She was floating in the lake."

"Are you going to investigate her death?" He lifted a thick white eyebrow in question.

"I'm not sure," I said.

"I'm certain you'll do the right thing whatever that turns out to be." He tipped his hat. "Have a good evening." And he was gone. Mal and I went down the alley toward the street. The crowds had dwindled, and the air was cool with that summer evening breeze.

I hurried toward the newspaper and ran into Liz locking up. Liz McElroy and her grandfather ran the *Town Crier*. "Wait!" I said.

"Hi, Allie," Liz said. She had curly hair and wore jeans and a T-shirt. "What's up? Do you have news of who killed Winona?"

"No news," I said with a sigh. Mal sniffed Liz's boots

while I stood face-to-face. "I wanted to put a help-wanted ad in the paper. I need someone to replace Sandy."

"Sure," she said. "Come on in." She unlocked the door and we both entered. Inside was cool and smelled of ink and paper. "How big of an ad do you want?"

"Just the usual help-wanted classified," I said. "I'm hoping a high school senior sees it or a college kid home for the summer."

"What about Sandy's family?" Liz said. "Haven't they done some work for you before?"

"They have," I said. "But I can't pay all that well, so I didn't want to ask them."

"Here's a sheet of paper," she said. "Write it up and I'll see it gets in tomorrow's paper."

"Thanks," I said. While I wrote, Liz picked up Mal and petted her.

"Any news on the killer?" Liz asked again.

"None," I said. "Just rumors so far."

"I'm betting it was the Alpines," she said. "They're fanatical when it comes to Natasha's pageant career. Are you going to investigate?"

"Not officially," I said. "But I might kick around a rumor or two."

"Well, keep me in the loop," she said. "A good murder is front page and Rex isn't sharing any information."

"I'll do my best to keep you up to date," I said and handed her the paper. "Thanks for letting me in late and posting the job."

"Of course," she said. "Anything for a friend, especially if you need me to bury a body."

Chapter 6

I doubted if I would ever need to bury a body, but Liz was a good friend and I believed she meant it as a joke. Just like I'd help her as well, should she ever need it. Mal and I walked down to Doud's to see if Mary Emry was still at work. I looked in the window and saw that Joan Bright was at the register. I picked up Mal and stepped into the store.

"No dogs in the store," Joan said as she spotted me.

"I was wondering if Mary Emry was still at work," I said, standing my ground. Mal was in my arms and a well-behaved dog, but I didn't want to get into too much trouble by putting her down.

"She went home at five," Joan said.

"Thanks," I replied and Mal and I left. I put my pup down and headed out to Mary's house.

Mary lived in an apartment above a T-shirt shop. We

went around to the back alley, climbed the metal stairs, and knocked on her door. She looked out her kitchen window and then opened the door. "Yes?"

"Hi, Mary," I said. "I was wondering if you had a few minutes to chat. I'll buy you a coffee."

She studied me for a long, awkward moment. "Sure," she said and closed the door. I assumed she was getting her purse. Mary was a quiet woman in her early forties with dark brown hair and brown eyes. She stepped out again, wearing a gray camp shirt and jeans.

"I thought we'd go to the Beanery on the marina since I have Mal with me," I said. Mal was in my arms and she licked my cheek at the sound of her name.

"Sure." Mary and I went down the stairs and walked in silence to the Beanery. Once there, we ordered drinks and I paid. Then found a round picnic table with an umbrella to sit under.

"Thanks for this," I said. "We never get a chance to really talk, and I thought this would be a good time."

"Okay," she said.

"What did you think of the Midsummer Night's Festival?" I asked as I petted Mal, who had jumped up into my lap.

"It raised money for a good cause," she said.

"Did you go to the bonfire? I was having so much fun dancing I didn't really pay attention to who all was there."

"For a while," she replied and sipped her drink. "I'm not big into large events. I prefer to be home with my cat, Memphis."

"Oh, what kind of cat is he? My own Mella is such a joy."

"He's a gray tabby," she said. "I've had him for twelve years now. I prefer his company to people."

"Well, I can certainly understand that," I said. "I bet you get a lot of handling people all day working at Doud's."

"Enough of people to just want to be home with my cat," she said. "I don't often get asked out for coffee drinks."

"I'm sorry," I said. "I should have done this sooner. I was wondering about the festival because Michelle Bell has asked me to join the committee and I wanted to know what people thought of it. I thought you might have a feel for the sentiment because of your job."

"I thought you might want to know what I know about Winona's murder," she said and gave me a pointed look.

I felt heat rush into my cheeks. "Well, that, too, if I'm to be honest. I overheard Gracie tell you that she heard Elias Sumner killed Winona. It was the first I'd heard of that theory."

"She did say that," Mary said. "It seems that Winona and Elias had a heated argument out in her front lawn that morning about her rosebushes. That woman was obsessed with her roses. She hired Elias to do her gardening while she worked on the festival and, according to the people who overheard the fight, he had put the wrong herbicide on them, and they were doing poorly."

"She fired him?" I asked.

"And threatened to ruin him as a gardener," Mary said. "You see, she entered her roses in the county fair every year and won championship after championship. She was so angry that he ruined that for her."

"Why would an experienced gardener use the wrong fertilizer?" I mused.

"Some people think he did it to get back at her for micromanaging his work." Mary sipped her coffee. "She wasn't satisfied unless she did something. Winona was a tough woman to work for."

"Do you think he did that on purpose? But it would ruin his reputation as a gardener," I pointed out. "Something else must have happened."

"Whatever it was, her roses don't matter now," Mary said. "And for the record, Elias wasn't the only one Winona pushed. She had a bad habit of stealing other people's ideas and making them her own."

"I didn't know her very well, but she doesn't sound all that great. Why was she in charge of the festival?"

"Because she was particularly good at project management and people knew they could count on her to get it done this year. And to answer your first question, the response to the festival was overwhelmingly positive, minus the fact that it ended with a bang."

"Literally," I said under my breath. "We should do this more often." I stood and put Mal on the ground. "Let's be friends."

"No, thanks," Mary said, got up, and threw her cup in the trash bin. "I'm happy just hanging out with Memphis. But, hey, if you ever need more gossip, come by. I like a good caramel macchiato."

"I'll remember that," I said and watched her walk off. "Well, Mal." I looked down at my dog. "That was informative. Let's go look at Winona's roses, shall we?"

Chocolate Rye Cookies

Ingredients:
¾ cup walnut halves
9 ounces bittersweet chocolate
1 cup baking cocoa
¾ cup unsalted butter
½ teaspoon vanilla extract
1½ cups sugar
4 large eggs, at room temperature
½ cup rye flour
½ teaspoon baking powder
½ teaspoon kosher salt
½ cup semisweet chocolate chips

Directions:
Preheat oven to 350 degrees F. Place walnuts on a cookie sheet and bake for 8–10 minutes. Let cool and chop into pieces and set aside.

Take 5 ounces of bittersweet chocolate and butter and microwave on high for 30 seconds. Add cocoa and stir until smooth. In a large bowl, whisk together sugar and eggs until light and fluffy. Add chocolate and butter mixture. Next, hand mix flour, baking powder, and salt and slowly add to sugar and egg mixture. Chop up remaining 4 ounces of bittersweet chocolate add it and the semisweet chocolate chips and stir.

Place the dough in an airtight container and refrigerate overnight.

Preheat oven to 350 degrees. On a parchment paper

lined cookie sheet, add dough in $\frac{1}{4}$ cup scoops 2 inches apart. Bake for 10–12 minutes until edges start to crack and middle is set.

Cool on wire rack. Store in airtight container. Makes 18. Enjoy!

Chapter 7

The thing about summer nights is that the sun stays out for a long time. It might be nearly seven in the evening, but there was enough light to view a garden. Mal and I walked up to Winona's two-story home with a big front porch. It was clad in brown shingles with cream trim. The yard was surrounded by a three-foot white picket fence and her gardens looked like something out of a magazine. Her lilacs were thick and still held a bloom or two. She had hibiscus, Shasta daisies, cornflowers, and more growing riotously. The colors were gorgeous. Even her lawn was thick and green.

"Well, Mal, this doesn't look like the gardener hurt anything." I opened the gate and we walked down the path to the side yard, where the rosebushes looked as if they had been burned. The leaves were all turning yellow. "Oh, no," I said, my heart sad at the look of them. "This really is bad."

"This is not my fault."

I turned to see Elias leaning on a hoe behind me. "Oh, you startled me."

"Didn't mean to," he said. "Just came back out myself to see if I could save the poor things."

"But Winona is dead," I pointed out.

"Doesn't mean I want to see beautiful roses lost." He started to hoe around them. "It looks like they were burned by an herbicide."

"Yes," I said. "I heard you and Winona had a fight about that."

"She wouldn't listen." He worked the topsoil away from the bushes. "I told her I didn't do it. She didn't believe me and fired me. But I stake my reputation on my work, so I had to come back."

"To the scene of the crime," I muttered.

He straightened. "I wouldn't do such a thing to plants and it doesn't matter if you believe me or not."

I took a step back. "I heard Winona was very difficult to work for."

"She was exacting and a micromanager," he said and went back to his work digging the soil out with the hoe. "But I've worked for her for years. Why suddenly turn on her? And if you're asking, yes, I do have an alibi for her death. I was with my sister Kate at the bonfire. She'll vouch for me."

"Right," I said. "I'm sorry to have assumed the worst. But do you think the roses were harmed deliberately?"

"Yes, I do," he said and walked over to where he put a wheelbarrow full of fresh dirt. "I'm going to have to dig them out and replace the dirt around the roots and replant. Then maybe they'll come back next year. I'm afraid they are toast this year."

"I heard they were grand champion roses," I said, trying a new tack. "Who did she beat out with her roses? Maybe that's why they were sabotaged."

"That would be Susan Gates and Kelly Miller," he said. "I do their gardening too. At least I did. Who knows now that rumors have me hurting plants."

"I promise not to spread any rumors," I said. "I'll even put a good word in for you. Do you think one of those ladies could have done this?"

"Maybe." He shrugged. "But Winona has been winning for years. Why would they have done this now? Why not years ago?"

"Well, you have a point there," I said. Mal barked and I looked up to see Rex coming our way.

"Allie, what brings you here?" Rex asked, his blue eyes glittering in the soft evening light.

"I heard about the roses and wondered if it was true," I said as Mal jumped up on him, looking for attention.

"Rex and I already talked." Elias straightened and looked Rex in the eye. "Did you talk to my sister?"

"I did," Rex said. "Your alibi holds up. I came out to go through Winona's house and look for clues to who might have killed her."

"Can I go with you?" I asked, but I knew the answer as the words left my mouth.

"No," he said. "This is official police business."

"Right," I said. "Okay, thanks for talking with me. Bye, guys." Mal and I moved across the lawn and out to the street. I could pop in and see if Susan or Kelly were home. Maybe they could shed some light on who might have tried to kill Winona's roses and if that was connected to her death.

Chapter 8

Susan Gates's home was about a half a mile from Winona's. A lovely 1920s bungalow, her picket fence, and glorious gardens rivaled Winona's. Mal and I walked by to find Susan out in her gardens, pulling weeds.

"Hello." I waved. "Your garden is gorgeous."

"Thank you!" She straightened, put her hands on her back, stretched, and came to the fence to chat. "Your dog is super-cute. It's Allie, right? I'm Susan."

"Yes," I said and held out my hand. "Nice to meet you, Susan. I hear you have champion roses."

"Not champion," she said wryly. "Only blue ribbon. Winona always was the champion."

"Not this year," I said.

"No." She shook her head. "It's sad, really."

"I heard someone put herbicide on her roses and burned them."

"What? That's tragic," Susan said. "I loved her roses."

"Do you know who might have wanted to keep her from winning this year's championship?"

"Well, I would love to win, but I wouldn't hurt roses. In fact, I don't know anyone who would do such a thing. Why? Do you think it's connected to Winona's death?"

I shook my head. "There's no telling," I said. "I just wondered. By the way, I talked to Elias Sumner and he didn't hurt the roses."

"I, for one, wouldn't have thought him capable of hurting a plant," she said. "He's one of the best gardeners. Loves his work as much as I love my garden."

"There's a rumor going around that he did hurt the roses because someone overheard him and Winona fighting over it. But he swears he didn't, so if you hear that he did, please squelch the idea."

"Of course, of course," she said.

"Great. I've got to run. It was nice meeting you and you really do have gorgeous gardens."

"Thanks," she said and waved to us with her gloved hands before going back to her weeding.

So that was a dead end. Whoever hurt Winona's roses was most likely not a gardener, I surmised. Which left nearly everyone else on the island as a suspect.

"We've got an applicant for the position you posted," Frances said the next morning when I came out of the fudge shop after finishing filling the counter.

"Wonderful," I said. "Who?"

"Madison Gimble. She's Deidre's girl and she's on the island for the summer," Frances said. "She's at Michigan State for college in the fall."

"Wonderful," I said. "Anyone else?"

"So far, no," Frances said. "I told Madison that she could come in this afternoon for an interview."

"Perfect," I said and took off my baker's hat. "I'm going to go up and shower off the candy. Do you need me for anything? How's the Westminster family doing?"

"I'm fine," Frances said. "The Westminsters are just great to have. It's nice to have a full hotel and everyone knowing everyone. Makes it happy."

"It sure does," I said. "Thanks to Jenn for booking so many events here."

"You also get credit for putting in the rooftop deck."

"Thanks," I said. "Yesterday's wedding and reception seemed to go off well. Jenn should be in today just to check in with the family."

"Some of them are leaving today but most are going tomorrow," Frances said. "They wanted an extra day to see the sights."

"Speaking of sights, I'm a mess. I'm running up for a shower and will be down shortly." I ran upstairs to shower and change. It was nice to be done with most of the candy making. I usually put on two demonstrations a day: one at eleven and one at two in the afternoon. It was always nice to have a fresh baker's coat and clean hair.

After the shower and blowing out my hair, I walked into the living room and heard a knock at my back door. Mal ran and barked and jumped on the door. I glanced out to see Patricia Ramsfeld. "Hello," I said, opening my door to the woman and the warm summer air.

"Oh, Allie, I'm glad I caught you at home. I was wondering if you might give me some advice," Patricia said.

"Certainly," I said. "Come on in." I picked up Mal and opened the door wide. Patricia came in. Today she wore a tunic and matching slacks. "Can I get you something to drink? Tea? Water?"

"Tea would be lovely."

She moved around the bar and took a seat at it. I put Mal down, washed my hands, and poured us both a glass of iced tea, then put out the sugar in case she wanted it. She took a long swallow of the tea. "Oh, goodness, that hits the spot."

"What can I do for you, Patricia?"

"I think I saw someone on the pier with Winona the night she was killed. I've been mulling over going to Rex because I can't be sure. It was dark and the only real thing I have to go on was they wore silver fairy wings. Do you think Rex would want to know that?"

"I think he would like any information you might have," I said.

"Even something so vague?"

"It might give him something new to go on," I said. "Do you remember who was wearing silver wings?"

"There were so many people there wearing wings," she said. "I couldn't tell you if they were a man or a woman."

"Were they taller or shorter than Winona?"

"A little shorter, I think." She fidgeted in her chair. "I could see the top of her head. I knew it was Winona because of her unique unicorn headdress. I mean, there were a lot of unicorns at the party, but hers stood out."

"It certainly did," I said. "Did you hear any voices? Could you tell if they were arguing?"

"Oh, goodness, no. I remember talking to Susan and caught a movement out of the corner of my eye. That's when I spied them. They were both gesturing with their arms, but then Susan asked me a question and I gave her my undivided attention. It's why I've been mulling it over. I mean, catching something from the corner of your eye in the dark is hardly something to say you witnessed."

"I think it's okay to take that to Rex." I sipped my tea. "If you're worried about bothering him, make an appointment. He takes those as well as just swinging by."

"That's a wonderful idea." She popped up off the barstool. "Thank you and thanks for the tea." She gave Mal a pat on the head, and I let her out the back door. "I feel so much better. I should have come to see you before now."

"I can understand your hesitation," I said. "Have a great day."

"I will. Bye now." She turned and walked down my staircase.

I closed the door and studied Mal. "Well, we know someone with silver wings was talking to Winona on the pier. My guess is it was most likely a woman. Therefore, it's safe to assume a woman was one of the last people to talk to Winona and may have been her killer."

Chapter 9

"Welcome to the McMurphy," I said to the young woman as I shook her hand. "I'm Allie and this is my general manager, Frances."

"So nice to meet you," Madison said and shook both our hands. She was a slight woman about five foot two with red hair and freckles across her nose.

"Thank you for answering our ad," I said. "Come have a seat." I waved her toward the sitting area near the coffee bar. She took a seat on the edge of a wing-back chair. "Let me tell you a bit about the job. I'm looking for someone to assist me in my twice-daily demonstrations and then to work the fudge shop. The job would be five days a week with Mondays and Tuesdays off. The hours are eleven a.m. to five p.m. with a thirty-minute lunch break. What do you think?"

"I think it sounds perfect," she said. "I got here late for

picking up other jobs, but it would be nice to earn some extra cash while I'm staying here this summer."

"Why don't you tell us a bit about yourself?" I asked. Frances nodded her agreement as she stood beside me.

"Well, I'm from Grand Rapids and I'm attending Michigan State for a degree in communications. I hope to work in Chicago one day for a big agency."

"Very nice," Frances said.

"Do you mind making minimum wage?" I asked. "I can keep you stocked in fudge."

She smiled. "I don't mind the salary and I may love fudge, but I'm going to do my best not to eat too much. Plus, I'm looking forward to learning how to make all the different fudges."

I stood. "Great, you're hired. When can you start?"

"Will tomorrow do?"

"Certainly," I said. "We can train you the next two days and then start you on your regular schedule."

"Sounds good."

"Wear comfortable pants or jeans and a white shirt. Polo shirts are fine, too. We'll see you at eleven?"

"Absolutely," she said. "It was so nice to meet you both." She shook our hands again and left.

"I think she'll work out very well," I said.

"She's no Sandy Everheart, but she'll do. I did check her references as well and they all spoke glowingly about her work."

"It will be nice to have some help around here," I said.

"Allie."

I turned to see Carol and Barbara Vissor coming through the lobby door. Carol was dressed in velour sweats and looked like she'd jogged the way to the Mc-Murphy. "Can we talk to you for a minute?"

"It's rather important," Barbara said. Her gray curls were perfectly set and she, too, wore sweats, only her sweatshirt said *My Grandma is the greatest*.

"Sure," I said. "Let's go up to my apartment. Can I get you some tea?"

"That would be wonderful," Barbara said.

I unbuttoned my baker's coat as we climbed the stairs. "The festival seemed to be a nice success. I've got a committee meeting later this afternoon to go over the final numbers, but it looked like we raised a good five thousand dollars for the kids."

"I agree," Carol said. "Winona did a great job. She would have loved to see how it all came together."

"It's just so tragic that she died so suddenly. We were the best of friends," Barbara huffed her way to the top of the steps.

"I'm so sorry for your loss," I said as we walked down the hall. I waved to Jenn in the office and then unlocked my apartment door. Mal had followed us up the stairs and raced inside to try and pounce on Mella. My cat jumped up on the cat tree and scowled down at the pup. I hung my coat and hat on the coatrack just inside the door.

"That's what we came to talk to you about." Carol took a seat in one of my barstools. Barbara followed suit. I pulled out three glasses, added ice, and poured iced tea into each.

"Sugar?" I asked.

"None for me," Barbara said.

"No, thank you," Carol said. "I'm a true northerner."

"Me too," I agreed and saluted them with my glass. "Now, what do you want to talk about?"

"This," Carol said and slid a folded piece of paper across the breakfast bar. I picked it up.

"What?" I unfolded it to see a typed message ranting about the pageant and how the festival committee had made a big mistake disqualifying Natasha. "Goodness."

"I know, right?" Barbara said. "Who would write such a thing? Read the back."

I turned it over and there in black-and-white was a threat: *Overturn your decision or you may end up just like Winona Higer.*

"That sounds dangerous," I said. "You need to take this to Rex right away."

"We brought it to you," Carol said. "Rex doesn't have time to figure out who wrote this, and I know you are busy, but I thought we could find the author on our own. You know, investigate it further before we go to the cops."

Barbara nodded her agreement.

"And do what?" I asked.

"Tell the perpetrator that threats won't change the outcome."

"Why would they care about the outcome of the pageant now that this is the last day of the festival?" I asked.

"Because the queen gets an automatic entry into the Miss Mackinac Island pageant that then goes on to the Miss Michigan pageant and eventually the Miss America pageant," Barbara said in one breath. "I researched it."

"Oh," I said. "But can't Natasha just enter the pageant on her own? Her family can pay for the entry."

"She needs a sponsor," Carol pointed out.

"Well, I can certainly sponsor Natasha if the writer of this note would like me to. Anything to help calm the situation down. Where did you get this?"

"It was slipped under my door," Carol said. "Quite unnerving to see it when we got to my house from our morning jog."

"I bet it was," I agreed. "Was anyone around? Did you see who might have left it?"

"No, there was no one around," Barbara said.

"But I'm certain it's those Alpine ladies." Carol was adamant. "Who else would be so incensed as to write a note? I wouldn't be surprised if they wrote a letter to the editor about it."

"Well, that's much better than leaving threats under people's doors," I said. "Give me a few minutes and I'll meet you downstairs. We'll go to the Alpines and put an end to this nonsense."

"Thank you, Allie," Carol said and finished her tea.

"We appreciate your help," Barbara said. "With your reputation for finding killers, they might actually come clean when we confront them."

"If only it were that simple," I said under my breath.

Chapter 10

Within a half hour, Carol, Barbara, and I were striding up to the Alpines' door. They lived in a huge Victorian mansion set up on the hill with a wonderful view of the straits of Mackinac. The wind blew pleasantly up here and all the windows to the house were open. A wind chime twinkled beautiful notes as I marched up the stairs and rang the doorbell.

The senior Mrs. Helen Alpine answered the door. "Yes? What do you want?"

"I'm Allie McMurphy and this is—"

"Carol Tunisian and Barbara Vissor. Yes, I'm aware of who you all are."

"May we come in?" I asked.

"Whatever for?" she asked as she stared down her nose at us.

"We were wondering if you wouldn't mind helping us solve a bit of a mystery," I said while Carol opened and closed her mouth like a fish out of water. I nudged her.

"What sort of mystery?" the elder woman asked.

"Someone stuck this note under Carol's door this morning," I said and handed her the missive. "Would you know who might have been so concerned for Natasha?"

"I understand that her disqualification came as quite a shock to her and your family, but I hope you understand it can't be reversed," Carol said. "If you are concerned about her entry into Miss Mackinac Island, then we have a proposition for you."

Helen scowled and handed us back the letter. "Are you accusing me or my family of writing this letter?"

"No, ma'am," I said. "We just want to let Natasha know that if she needs any sponsorship to enter the Miss Mackinac Island contest, I will gladly have the McMurphy Hotel and Fudge Shop sponsor her."

"We don't need your hotel sponsorship," Helen said. "Good day, ladies."

"Wait!"

She shut the door on us. I looked at Carol and Barbara and shrugged. "We tried."

"But she didn't address the threat," Carol said. "I'm not comfortable going home until the threat is dealt with."

"Then you need to take it to Rex," I said as we stepped off the porch. I glanced behind to see Helen drop the curtain so I wouldn't know she had been watching us.

Barbara's mouth moved into a thin line. "With the murder investigation, we just don't think that Rex will give it the attention it deserves."

"I'll talk to him about it," I said. "We have a dinner date tonight if he's not too busy."

"You two are certainly seeing a lot of each other lately," Carol noted with a gleam in her eye.

"We're dating," I said. "I'm not sure where it's going, but I'm enjoying the journey."

"Everyone knows that Rex is looking for a woman who will settle down on the island," Barbara said.

"And I plan on settling down here," I said. "I rather enjoyed my first winter. It was nice and quiet and my on-line fudge sales kept me occupied. Plus, I'm young enough not to want to be a snowbird."

"I wish I were a snowbird." Barbara stepped down off the porch. "It would be fun to go south to Texas or Florida for the winters."

"Why aren't you?" I asked.

"My husband Barry isn't interested in going to either place. He has lived his entire life here and this is where he always wants to be. Still, my old joints sure would like warmer weather in January and February."

"You should get your girlfriends together and go for a week each year," I suggested.

"As long as we can get off the island," she said. "I'm not big on private airplanes."

"Even if Sophie is flying?" Sophie was a good friend, and a pilot who flew people on and off the island as both a charter and for the Grand Hotel.

"Even then," Barbara said with a shake of her head. "I was in a small plane once. I won't make that mistake twice. I'm afraid of heights."

"I see," I said. "So go by ferry. They have the Coast Guard come and cut through the ice. We aren't always icebound."

"You're right," Carol said. "We should do it, Barbara. I'll talk to Edith and Irene."

"In the meantime, let me have that letter and I'll talk to Rex about it."

"Okay," Carol said. "But any further threats and I'm writing a letter to the editor myself."

"You do that," I said. I left Carol and Barbara at the back door to the McMurphy and went inside. Mal greeted me at the door with a bark and slid into my shins. I picked her up and gave her a quick squeeze until she yelped. I put her down and let Frances know I was taking her for a walk. I slipped her halter on and connected her leash. Then we went out the back.

Mal ran across the alley to a small patch of grass that backed up against the fence to a hotel on the other side. I stood with her until I spotted Mr. Beecher walking down the alley.

"Hello, Allie," he called with a wave. His left hand held tight to a cane as he walked. He wore a hat, a waist-coat and suit coat, along with wool pants. He was quite dapper.

"Hello, Mr. Beecher, how are you? Were you able to get out and enjoy the end of the festival today?"

"I most certainly did," he said and Mal jumped up and pirouetted for her treat. He gave it to her and smiled up at me as he straightened. "Like I said yesterday, I think the festival was a complete success. The ladies did very well with it. How's the investigation into Winona's death going?"

"I thought it was best to let Rex handle it, but then Mrs. Tunisian got a threatening note." I took the note out of my sweater pocket and handed it to him. "Now I think I may need to be more involved."

"Wow, this is unkind," he said as he read it.

"Read the back," I said. "It's a threat."

"I don't understand what the writer of the note wants. What's done is done. There's very little this threat will accomplish."

"We took it to the Alpines and asked if we could talk it over."

"That seems like the right thing to do," he said. "Very levelheaded."

"Helen denied that it was written by anyone in their family," I said. "So, now Mal and I are taking it to Rex."

"The Alpines didn't write it? I wonder who else was so involved with Natasha?" Mr. Beecher handed me the letter. "Sounds like you do have a mystery on your hands. If anyone can figure out the answer, it's you, young lady."

"Thanks for the vote of confidence," I said and tucked the letter back into my pocket. Now all I had to do was make good on the promise.

Chapter 11

"Thank you for bringing the note to me this afternoon, but I'm not sure there's anything the police can do," Rex said as he sat across from me at the dinner table.

"You don't think it's tied to Winona's death?" I asked, leaning toward him. We sat at the tiny dining table for two that was in my apartment on the other side of the breakfast bar from the kitchen. I had made lasagna and Rex brought over a loaf of garlic bread and a bottle of red wine.

"Well, the author certainly wants you to think it's related," Rex said. "But without knowing who wrote it and why, there's no real knowing if it's a credible threat or not."

"That's what I thought," I said and leaned back in my chair. "We took it to the Alpines, but Helen said she had no idea where it came from. She also dismissed my offer to sponsor Natasha in the Miss Mackinac Contest."

"What do those two things have to do with each other?" Rex asked and sipped his wine. I explained how the pageants fed into one another.

"You see, the Miss Mackinac pageant is the only reason we could come up with that someone would want to reinstate Natasha. I mean, the parade is over and as of tonight, so is the festival."

"I suppose that makes some sort of sense," he said and took his last bite of lasagna. "Even still, I can't pin any of this on Natasha or her relatives. There's just no proof. And they denied it to your face."

"She could have been lying," I said and drummed my fingers on the table. "Or Natasha or her mother Belinda wrote it, and Helen didn't know."

"Well, if she didn't know, she certainly does now," Rex said. "I tell you what: I'll keep the note for now. Maybe it will play a role in putting the killer away."

"Good," I said and blew out a long breath, then stabbed my remaining lasagna with my fork. "How's the investigation going? Any new leads?"

"I really can't say," he said. "Except it's going."

"Did you find anything further at Winona's home?" I put a bite of lasagna in my mouth. It was filled with the flavor of tomato, ground beef, oregano, and ricotta cheese.

"You know I couldn't tell you if I did. But what I can tell you is that Elias's alibi checked out, so he's no longer a suspect."

"Someone poisoned Winona's prize roses," I said. "Do you think the two things are related?"

"They could be," he said. "But not very likely. Killing

roses is premeditated. I think that Winona was killed in the heat of the moment. Why else risk killing her with so many people around?"

"It's just strange that both things happened on the same day." I stood and picked up our plates, taking them to the sink.

"At this point I can't rule anything out," he said. "Listen, I do want to say, I'm glad you aren't investigating this one," he said. "It's best if we aren't at odds with each other."

I shrugged. "I don't have a real reason to investigate," I said. "No one I love is in danger."

"Let's hope it stays that way."

Chapter 12

The next morning after I finished filling the counter with fudge, I took Mal for a walk before I had to spend the day training Madison. We went down to the beach to try to look again at the spot where I pulled Winona out of the water. I watched as the waves moved in and out with the breeze. Throwing a stick out into the surf, I waited to see if it moved to the left as it rolled in and out. Mal barked when I threw it, but she wasn't a fan of the water, so she didn't go chasing it.

"Let's see how far the stick floats," I said to Mal. "It's not body-size but it could give us a better idea where Winona was murdered."

The stick floated in and out but didn't go sideways. I didn't know much about currents, but I thought perhaps that meant that Winona was killed here. I chewed on that thought a moment. She had been floating pretty far out, I was up to my chest in water when I got her, and a body is heavy. So maybe she was killed on the pier where Patricia saw her talking to someone with silver fairy wings.

Mal and I walked the beach to the point of the bonfire. There was an old pier halfway from the bonfire to the murder scene. It was obstructed by the makeshift stage that had been built for the band and the pageant. Mal and I walked the pier and I imagined Winona in a fight with the killer. I'm certain it would have been heard by somebody. I tossed another stick in the water. This time it floated away from the pier and toward the shore.

"So, Mal, this is most likely where Winona was shot," I said.

"Allie?"

I nearly jumped out of my skin at the sound of my name. I whirled around to see Michelle at the end of the pier. "Oh," I said my hand on my racing heart. "You scared me."

"I didn't mean to," Michelle said. Michelle was smaller than me and just a few years older than Natasha. She had been Winona's right-hand girl, assisting the woman in all things pageant and festival. "I saw you standing out here alone and wondered what you were doing. Are you looking for Winona's killer?"

"Oh," I said and smiled. "No, I'm leaving that up to Rex this time. I was just out walking Mal and saw the pier and thought it would be a nice view of the beach." Which wasn't exactly a lie.

She tilted her head and her long black hair fell like a curtain to the side.

"Oh, yeah," she said. "I forget you're new to the island. We used to play on this pier, Natasha and me and our friend Brianna. It's just long enough to be a nice pretend fort. The boys were always jealous that we got here first."

I smiled. "I bet they were. Do you know when they are going to take down the stage?" I pointed to the structure that blocked the view of the pier.

"Today," she said. "It's why I'm here. Ethan is bringing a crew to disassemble it."

"Disassemble it?"

"Yes," she said and pointed to the stage. "It's constructed to be movable, so we use it for all kinds of festivals and other things where we need a stage for the speaker or a band. Say, your friend Jenn plans weddings, right?"

"Yes," I said.

"Tell her she can rent the stage anytime she wants for a wedding anywhere on the island. It's only a hundred dollars for setup and teardown."

"Cool," I said. "I'll tell her."

Ethan and a gang of young men came walking down the path toward us. They were rowdy and jostled each other.

"Well, I'd better let you go," I said and then paused. "One quick question."

"Okay?"

"Do you know who might have wanted to kill Winona? Did you see anything that night?"

"Oh gosh, I have no idea who would do such a terrible thing. She was the best boss ever," Michelle said. "And I didn't see anything because I got a headache and went home shortly before the fireworks started. My mother can verify that, and I already told Rex."

"I'm sorry for your loss," I said. "Thanks for letting me know."

"My pleasure," she said. "Oh, and thanks for stepping up and volunteering for next year's festival. We can always use good volunteers."

"Sure," I said. "It sounds like it will be fun."

"And a whole lot of work," she warned. "Anyway, I need to go supervise these guys before they get out of hand."

Mal and I walked up the beach and headed back home. I was quite sure whoever shot Winona had done it off the pier. Now all I needed was the identity of the person in silver fairy wings. If they weren't the killer, they might have seen who was.

I was lost in thought when Mal and I cut through the schoolyard to Main Street. Suddenly my pup started sniffing like Scooby-Doo. "Mal," I said. "What is it?"

She pulled me forward and toward a large patch of lilac bushes across the street from the school. We got to the lilacs and she wiggled her way between the bushes.

"Mal, stop it," I said and got down on my knees to pull her out. When I did, something caught my eye. Was that a ladies' dress pump? I pulled Mal toward me and in her mouth was a piece of cloth and it had a red stain in the corner that looked suspiciously like blood. "Oh, that's not good," I muttered and stood up with Mal in my hand and parted the bush. There was a woman lying with her legs in unnatural places and a large hole in the back of her head.

The killer had struck again.

Bourbon Cherry Pie

Ingredients:

2 9-inch pie crusts (one for the bottom and one for the top)

3 16-ounce bags of dark, sweet frozen cherries (tart will work, too).

¼ cup bourbon

½ cup sugar

3 tablespoons of cornstarch

3 tablespoons of lemon juice

Directions:

Thaw cherries, then in a large bowl mix cherries and bourbon (to taste) and soak overnight.

Preheat oven to 350 degrees F. Place one crust in a 9-inch pan and place the pan on a baking sheet.

Drain cherries and add sugar, cornstarch, and lemon juice and mix to coat the cherries. Pour into pie pan. Add second crust on top and cut vents in the top crust or if you're feeling fancy, create a lattice top. Bake until crust is a deep golden brown and the juice begins to ooze about 1¼ –1½ hours. Remove and let pie cool completely. Serve with vanilla ice cream and enjoy!

Chapter 13

"This is 911, what's your emergency?"

"Charlene, I need to report a dead body," I said. "I'm across from the school building."

"Oh, dear," she said. "Police and ambulance are on their way. Do you know for sure they are dead?"

"Yes, there's quite a large exit wound in the back of her head."

"Do you recognize her?" Charlene asked breathlessly.

"She's face down," I said. "And lying in a bush. So no, I don't recognize her right offhand."

In the distance I heard the wail of the sirens. I turned to see two police officers on bikes tearing up the road toward me.

"I see the officers," I said.

"Are you safe?" she asked.

I glanced around as Mal squirmed in my arms. "Yes, I think so."

"Then I'll go ahead and hang up."

Rex and Charles arrived in tandem.

"What do we have?" Rex asked as he kickstanded his bike and pulled off his helmet.

"A dead woman," I said. "Mal found her in the lilacs." I pointed to the bush and let him and Charles pull the branches back.

Rex said something dark under his breath. Charles took my elbow and walked me across the street.

"It's best if you stay here," he said. "I'll be putting up crime scene tape in a moment."

"Sure, thing," I said. "Oh, Mal had this in her mouth." I handed him the fabric that matched the woman's dress.

"Right." He pulled out an evidence bag, opened it, and I put the fabric inside. "Okay, you know the drill. Don't say anything to anyone until Rex gets back to you."

"Right," I said as I watched him walk away toward his bike and pull a roll of crime scene tape from one of his bike pouches.

"What's going on?" Liz walked up to me. Today she had on a lightweight camp shirt and pair of jeans. Her curly hair was pulled back into a single ponytail.

"Mal found a body." I held Mal in my arms and she sat up, enjoying the view from that height.

"Good dog!" Liz said and pulled out her notebook. "Who is it? How did Mal find it?"

"You know I can't talk to you until I talk to Rex," I said and noticed a crowd forming as Charles wound crime scene tape around a decent perimeter. The ambulance showed up and George stepped out with his kit in hand. I wanted to say, "You won't need it," but then I remembered I wasn't supposed to say anything. Liz already knew too much.

Officer Megan Lasko arrived next, parked her bike, and began talking to the crowd. "All right, folks. There's nothing to see here. Go on about your day." She scowled at them until the crowd thinned and only the hardy few stayed behind.

Charles lifted the tape and George got back into the ambulance and rolled it between the crowd and the lilac bush, effectively cutting off the crowd's view.

Several people protested the move, but Megan wasn't having any nonsense. "Go on home. You'll learn things as fast as we do. I'm sure Liz will be on the ball reporting this. Won't you, Liz?"

"Yes, I will," Liz addressed the crowd. "You can read all about it tomorrow morning in the *Town Crier.* We bring you accurate news."

The crowd moaned but slowly moved away. Shane arrived, carrying his crime scene kit. Mal and I waited while he processed the scene. The body was put into a big black bag and into the back of the ambulance to go to the morgue in St. Ignace.

"What time is it?" I asked Liz.

"After one," she replied.

"Oh, boy, I need to text Frances." I pulled out my phone. "She must be wondering where we are." Not to mention I was supposed to be training Madison and I had a demonstration in less than an hour.

"I'm sure she knows by now," Liz said. "I saw Irma Gooseman in the crowd. She'll be sure all the seniors know."

"I'll text her anyway," I said. "She needs to hear it from me." I opened my text screen and typed. **Frances, Mal and I found a dead body. I'll be here for a while until Rex releases me. Can you train Madison on the cash register?**

She texted back. **I have been. Figured you got hung up.**

It was another hour and even Liz had left after getting Officer Brown to promise her a statement before the end of the night. It was past my demo time and the officers were pacing the crime scene one foot at a time. I don't know what they were finding, but they'd been at it a long time and Mal and I were getting chilled by the cool breeze off the lake.

"Sorry that took so long," Rex said. "You look cold. Let's go back to the office and I can get you some coffee."

"Sounds good," I said. "My phone says the windchill makes it feel like sixty degrees." I rubbed my forearms. "Not exactly cold out, but cool for summer."

Mal and I walked with Rex to the police department. The white building held all kinds of government offices, including the police. We stepped inside and out of the wind. Rex took us back to an interrogation room and showed me a seat. Mal jumped up onto my lap and I petted her. Rex came back shortly with two coffees in hand.

"Creamer, no sugar, right?"

"Right," I replied.

He sat and took a sip himself. "Okay, I'm going to record this."

"That's fine," I said.

"This is Officer Manning with Allie McMurphy. Can you tell me what happened?"

I went over how Mal and I were coming back from our walk on the beach and how Mal found the victim. "Do you know who she was?"

"It was Patricia Ramsfeld," he said.

"Oh my gosh! Did she get in to tell you what she saw the night Winona was murdered?"

"She made an appointment for this afternoon." He raised an eyebrow. "She told you what she saw?"

"She was worried that it was too insignificant and came to me to see if I thought you should know. I told her to see you."

"She hadn't yet." He frowned. "What did she see?"

"She said she saw Winona talking to a person wearing what looked like silver fairy wings. They were on the pier."

"Why didn't she say that sooner?"

"She caught it out of the corner of her eye and thought it wouldn't help you as a witness."

"Maybe, maybe not," he said. "She should have come forward the very next day."

"People just want to stay out of your way," I said. "Besides, I think there were a lot of silver-looking fairy wings at the ball."

"Maybe she recognized the killer and was murdered for it before she could say anything to me," he mused.

"Or maybe she was killed because she's another member of the festival committee. She was vice chairman, along with Carol Tunisian. And Carol got that threat—"

"I'm going to cut you off right there," he said and held up his hand. "I sent patrolmen over to Mrs. Tunisian's house and she's fine."

"You'll have a patrol around her house until the killer is caught, right?" I asked and squeezed Mal.

"Right."

"What about Michelle Bell? She was Winona's assistant and is now chair of the committee. Also, Amy? Amy Houseman? She wasn't a committee member, but she was one of the parade judges."

"I'll send someone over to check on them as soon as we're done here," he said and wrote down a note.

"Who would do such a thing?" I asked. "And why did no one hear the gunshot? This time there were no fireworks to cover the sound."

"Only the cannon," he pointed out. Fort Mackinac sat on top of the hill facing the marina and held reenactments of the War of 1812 and shot off a cannon on the hour. I was so used to the sound I didn't notice.

"That means this was well planned," I said. "Not a crime of passion."

"Still most likely the same killer," he said.

"I was thinking Winona was killed for something she said, but now Patricia . . . Do you think it's connected to the pageant like Carol's note, or do you think it's something else?"

"I'm going to treat it like a separate incident until I know otherwise."

"You mean if the bullets match to the same gun," I concluded.

"Yes, that's what took us so long. We had real trouble finding the bullet. She had a clear exit wound and we had hoped to match bullets. My next thought is maybe she was killed somewhere else and dumped in that bush."

"But you found the bullet?"

"No," he said. "But we won't stop looking. Shane is taking the evidence we have back to the lab in St. Ignace to see if we can connect the two murders or we have two murderers on the island."

"I hate to say it, but I sure hope it's only one murderer. They have to be someone local," I said. "This feels like someone was mad about the festival and a fudgy wouldn't have any reason to be mad."

"Right now, the festival is the only connection between the two," he agreed. "Patricia really didn't witness anything that could lead us to the killer. So, for now, we're going to treat it like they are two separate cases."

"Still, now I'm really worried for Carol, Michelle, and Amy. Especially after Carol got that threat."

"We'll have patrol watching over everyone," he tried to reassure me.

"Okay," I said. "I guess I need to accept that."

"Please do," he said. "I don't want you to get hurt trying to find the killer."

"I won't get hurt," I said with my fingers crossed behind my back.

"Does that mean you won't investigate?"

"You know I can't promise you that," I said. "I have connections. The seniors might know something."

Rex blew out a long breath and rubbed his hand across his face in resignation. "Just be careful. If you think you've found the killer, please come to me first before you go trying to find hard proof."

"But you can't do anything without hard proof, right? We don't want to jeopardize your case or have you called out for harassment."

"But I can't have you putting your life in danger," he said.

"I won't," I said.

"Allie . . ."

"Well, I'll try really hard not to."

He sighed. "I guess that's all I can ask at this point." Then he reached over and squeezed my hand. "You and Mal can go home now. I won't be over for dinner; there's just too much paperwork to do."

"And a killer to catch," I said and stood.

"Yes," he said and stood as well. He gave me a soft, fast kiss and shepherded me through the bullpen to the front door.

"What can I tell Liz?"

He looked thoughtful. "You can tell her anything," he said. "Except how Patricia was killed. Let's keep that between us for now. Okay?"

"Okay." I kissed him again for good measure and Mal and I stepped out into the late afternoon. Rex didn't want me to investigate, but he also knew that I was going to do it anyway. I liked that he knows I'm my own person and can make my own decisions. Now all I had to do is figure out who would want both women dead and why. Two killers was not reasonable. At least that's what I hoped.

Chapter 14

The next morning was spent making fudge. Madison had agreed to come for a second training day, forfeiting her days off. I showed her how to help me with my ten o'clock demonstration and how to work the cash register. She picked up on things very quickly and was a lot of fun to work with.

"I'm going to leave you on your own," I said and moved out of the fudge shop. "Frances is here if you have any questions."

"Got it," Madison said.

After I showered and changed, I came down to see Frances. "I'm going to go see Carol," I said to Frances as she worked the registration desk. The next wedding party started to come in today for the Friday-night festivities and Jenn was running around with last-minute touches. But my mind was on the committee members.

"Be safe," Frances said. "You were gone a long time yesterday."

"I'm hoping Carol can help me figure out the who and the why of this situation. The killer has to be someone she knows."

"But if she's a target, you could get hurt along with her," Frances pointed out. "So be careful."

"I will," I said and left through the back door. I'd left Mal with Frances. If I was going to do some sleuthing, I didn't want my pup to get hurt, no matter how good her nose was at finding clues.

"Allie, wait up!"

I turned to see Amy coming toward me with a wave. "Hi, Amy. How are you?"

"I was looking for you and Frances said you were on your way to Carol's house?"

"Yes, to check on her, and check on you as well. Carol got a threatening note under her door the other day and I'm worried the killer is after the entire committee."

"Oh dear, a threatening note? That's terrible," she said.

"It threatened the ladies of the festival committee and then I found Patricia dead and now I'm really worried."

"Well, don't worry about me, I'm fit as a fiddle," Amy said. "But I was wondering if I could buy you a coffee. I have something I need your help with."

"Sure," I said.

She walked with me to the Beanery, but it was hopping at lunchtime, so we got our coffees and found a bench near the marina.

"What can I help you with?" I asked.

"This is terrible to ask, but I was wondering if you could do some sleuthing for me," she said. "Everyone knows how good you are at sniffing out bad behaviors."

"Sleuthing for what? Has someone else been murdered?"

"Not yet, but he's going to be," she said. "It's my husband. I think he's having an affair and I was wondering if you would help me find out if it's true or not. I know it's not what you do, but I'm really desperate here. He's gone three nights a week and tells me he's working overtime, but I'm not sure I believe him." Tears came to her eyes.

"Oh, honey, I'm sorry," I said and gave her a hug. "I'm sure it's nothing. Mackinac is a small place. If he's having an affair, someone's going to know about it."

"That's why I thought of you. You have connections to people that might be able to help."

"I tell you what," I said. "I'll ask around for you and see what I can come up with and I'll be discreet."

"Thank you so much," she said. "It will be a relief to find out the truth."

"Have you asked him? I know that sounds simplistic, but sometimes confronting people with the question gets you a true answer."

"I've asked him," she said. "He said he was working late."

"Where does he work?"

"He works at the stables," she answered. "He's a blacksmith part-time and then he works the ferries part-time as a driver."

"Well, you can be sure he's at work if he's working the ferries," I said. "But blacksmithing might be where he's not exactly telling the truth. When does he work late next?"

"Wednesday," she said. "He'll go straight from the ferry docks to the stable."

"We can do a stakeout," I suggested. "You know, follow him and see what he does."

"You would do that for me?"

"I would," I said. "But the thing is, there's a killer out there who may be targeting the festival committee, so please stay home and stay safe in the meantime. Okay? Promise me you'll not venture out on your own before then."

"I promise." She hugged me. "Thank you, I didn't know what to do."

"I'll ask around, too. Someone might know something." I stood. "I'm going to go check on Carol and Michelle."

"I saw Michelle at the administration building," Amy said. "She looked fine to me."

"Great, if you see her again, can you tell her about the threat and ask her to notify the police if she wants someone to go by her house at night."

"I'll tell her," Amy said.

I walked off toward Carol's house thinking about Amy's request. I'd never sleuthed out a cheating spouse before and I certainly hoped Amy was ready for whatever we found out.

Salted Caramel White Chocolate Fudge

Ingredients:
3 cups of white chocolate chips
1 14-ounce can of sweetened condensed milk
4 tablespoons of butter
1 teaspoon vanilla extract
Optional: 1 cup of chopped pecans
1 cup of room temperature caramel sauce (The kind you
   might put on ice cream.)
1 teaspoon coarse grain sea salt

Directions:
Line an 8x8-inch pan with buttered parchment paper. In a microwave safe bowl, combine white chocolate chips and sweetened condensed milk. Microwave on high for 30 seconds, stir. Repeat until the chips are nearly all melted. Stir until smooth. Add butter and vanilla and combine until smooth. Add nuts if desired. Pour into pan. Then place the room temperature caramel in a decorating bag. Make crisscrossed lines over the fudge. Use a knife to swirl the caramel into the fudge. Add a sprinkling of salt. Cool in the refrigerator. Cut into one-inch slices. Makes 64. Enjoy!

Chapter 15

The walk to Carol's house was breezy and warmer than the night before. My light sweater was all I needed.

"Allie," Irma Gooseman called after me. "Yoo-hoo, Allie!"

I stopped and turned around and watched as the older woman rushed to catch up with me. She wore an exercise outfit and running shoes, so it didn't take her long. "Hello, Irma."

"How are you, Allie? I understand you found Patricia dead yesterday. It must have been quite a shock."

"It was," I said. "Have you talked to Carol?"

"About that dreadful note? I certainly have," Irma said with a shake of her head. "I heard they have a policeman coming by her place every hour or so to make sure she is safe. Do you think the two things are connected?"

"Well," I said and walked up the hill toward Carol's home. "I don't think there's such a thing as coincidence. I'm guessing that the festival committee is being targeted, starting with the chair and vice chairs."

"Oh, dear, I'm suddenly glad I didn't volunteer for this committee. You see, I was visiting my daughter the first two weeks the committee started making plans. Not exactly a good time to be on a committee."

"No, I suppose it's not," I said. "Have you seen Carol? Do you know how she's holding up?"

"I was headed that way when I saw you," Irma said. "I missed her on her daily walk, so I figured it wouldn't hurt to drop in for a cup of coffee."

"I was thinking the same," I said. We approached Carol's bungalow. I climbed the three short steps and walked onto the white porch with the ceiling painted sky blue. Irma hurried behind me and reached out to knock on the door.

"Carol, are you home, dear?"

I saw the curtains in the front room move and then Carol opened the door. "Hi, ladies," Carol said. "Please come in."

We stepped inside. I took off my shoes and left them by the door and followed the two senior ladies through the front parlor, dining area, and into the kitchen in the back.

"I hope you have some coffee cake," Irma said as she sat down. "All this running has really worked up an appetite."

"I made one this morning," Carol said. "Allie, honey, sit down. There are four chairs. I've got coffee ready."

I sat and watched Carol pull out three thick mugs and pour in the richly scented brew.

"I know Irma and I take ours with sugar and cream. What do you like in your coffee, Allie?"

"I like cream," I said.

She put the three mugs on the table and then rummaged through the cupboards until she found a sugar bowl and creamer. She filled the creamer with milk and put them both on the table.

"Carol, you still don't have any of the pink packets?" Irma asked.

"Sugar is good for the body," Carol said. "You don't need all that artificial stuff." Then she pulled a cake stand off the counter, opened the metal top to display a sweet cinnamon ring of cake with blueberries embedded inside.

"Can I help you with the cake?" I asked.

"Sit down, Allie, it's no trouble at all," Carol said. Within minutes she had cake slices cut and served and sat with us stirring sugar and cream in her coffee. "I'm sure you're both here to check up on me after Patricia's death."

"Allie found her," Irma said. "Allie, how was she killed? Just like Winona?"

"I shouldn't say how she was killed," I said. "Just that she was and that Mal and I found her in the lilac bushes across from the school."

"But we're sure that the killer is bumping off members of the committee and that means you're in danger, Carol," Irma said.

"The police have been by the house nearly every hour," Carol said. "I'm fine. I have my doors and windows locked. Besides, now that Allie is on the committee, she's in as much danger as I am."

"But it sounds like you are a prisoner in your own home," I said. "I don't like it. We need to find out who is killing members of the committee and why."

"Well, we know why," Irma said. "They're mad because Natasha didn't win the queen title."

"I'm not sure," I hedged. "What if someone wants us to believe that?"

"It's the Alpines," Irma concluded. "They think the sun rises and sets with that Natasha. Did you see how horrified they were when she was disqualified?"

"It would seem if it were the Alpines, they would be mad at the auditors who audited the ballots and the information," I said. "By the way, how did they come to discover the lapse in community service hours? I mean, weren't they all signed for and verified before the end of the pageant?"

"No," Carol said. "There was a delay because Percy Miners was out sick. They only got the results the night of the announcement."

"I don't think that the Alpines would just murder people because they're mad," I said. "It doesn't make any sense."

"Yes, well, you don't know them like we do," Irma said. "If anyone is capable of murder, it's them."

"We went and talked to Helen," I pointed out. "It would be stupid of them to murder again, knowing that Carol and I both went to the house and offered a truce."

"A truce?" Irma said.

"Yes," I went on. "We figured that they were mad because Natasha needed a sponsor for the Miss Mackinac Island pageant, and I offered to have the McMurphy sponsor her."

"And Helen turned us down flat," Carol said. "She said that they didn't need our pity sponsorship . . . or something along those lines."

"Well," Irma said and sat back. "Well, if it's not the

Alpines, who is it? According to everyone, the festival was a huge success. Why kill committee members now?"

"Maybe it's not festival related," I posited.

"It's true," Carol said. "Only my note mentions the pageant. What else were Winona and Patricia working on?"

"We need to really dive into both women's lives and see where they connect," I said.

"Irma and I will gather information from the seniors," Carol said. "What are you going to do?"

"I'm going to talk to the Chamber of Commerce and see what other festival ideas were running through Winona and Patricia's heads and what other committees they were on."

"Sounds good," Carol said. "We'll meet back here in two days."

"Perfect," I said. "I've got one more question. Have you heard anything about Amy's husband Rick having an affair? Mackinac is a small island and I thought someone might have said something."

"No," Carol said. "I haven't. Have you, Irma?"

"Not a thing," Irma said. "As far as I know he and Amy are happily married."

"Okay, well, if you hear anything, would you let me know?"

"Certainly," they both agreed.

"Good, I've got some work to do at the McMurphy so it might take me some time to gather data about Winona and Patricia. But I'll head out to check on Michelle and then hit up the Chamber of Commerce from there." I stood. "Thanks for the coffee and cake."

"You didn't eat near enough. I'll cut you off a chunk to take back for your gang at the McMurphy. I know at the very least Rex could use some fattening up."

"I think he looks pretty good as he is now," Irma said and winked at me. "Wish I was about thirty years younger."

I shook my head. "No comments on my love life, okay?"

"I wasn't commenting on your love life," Irma said and raised her hands in surrender. "I was talking about Officer Manning's fine physique."

"Don't mind her," Carol said and handed me a plate full of the rich cake. "Take this back to the McMurphy. It's too much for me alone."

"Thanks," I said and left the house through the back door. Carol didn't have a fenced yard. Probably because she had an indoor cat and didn't need to fence her yard. I stepped out of the yard and to the street when I saw Charles ride by on his bike. He nodded at me and I waved back as best I could with a platter full of cake in my hand. At least they were looking out for Carol. If the festival was the reason for the killer to attack, it was best if Carol was looked after.

Chapter 16

After I dropped the cake off with a hungry Douglas and smiling Frances, I went straight to Michelle's house. She lived in a large Victorian cottage with gorgeous gardens of flowers spilling over into a green lawn. I knocked on the door and she answered. "Allie, what brings you here?"

"I came to check on you," I said. "Wow, your home is beautiful. Is it your family home?"

There was a curved wraparound porch and a bright white turret with blue and green accents.

"Yes, it's been in my family over one hundred years. Please," she said. "Come in. Can I get you anything?"

"Oh, I'm good," I said as I stepped into the large, paneled foyer painted an airy white. "How long has your family lived on the island?"

"We've been here since 1899," she said. "My great-grandfather was a wealthy merchant from Chicago, and they came out here for the summers to get away from the city heat."

She walked me into the front parlor with lush carpet and pale blue settee. "Have a seat."

"Thank you," I said. "I really came to make sure you are all right."

"Why wouldn't I be?" She wrinkled her brow.

"Someone slipped a threatening note under Carol Tunisian's door."

"Oh, dear, poor thing," she said and touched her throat. "Is she all right?"

"She's fine, but the note did threaten everyone on the committee and the next day Patricia was murdered."

"I heard," she said with her eyes wide. "I heard you found her. Are you all right? It had to be a fright."

"It was not fun. It's never fun to find a dead human being. The thing is, I just spoke to her and then I found her dead. It's all sort of surreal."

"Let me get you some water." She stood. "Sit and relax a moment."

She walked through what appeared to be a den and disappeared into the back of the house. I looked around at the opulence of the building. It was definitely old like the McMurphy, but had good bones that withstood the test of time.

"Here you go," she said and handed me the water. "I understand that you're worried that I'm in danger because I'm on the committee."

"Yes," I said. "I've talked to Rex and he's going to have police come by your home to ensure you are safe."

"Oh, good! To be frank, I'm kind of nervous about this." She paused thoughtfully and sipped her water.

"I've never been threatened before. What did the note say?"

"It said that they were angry because Natasha Alpine was disqualified, and that the entire committee should watch out. Then Patricia was killed, so it's best if you're not alone."

"I agree," she said. "Maybe I should call my mom and see if she won't come stay with me for a while until you get this sorted out."

"Where is she now?" I asked.

"In Chicago, but she could be here by tomorrow if I need her," Michelle said. I noted that her hand trembled.

I reached over and covered her hand with mine. "I think that's a good idea and don't worry, like I said, the police will be patrolling."

"Do you have any idea who the killer is? I know you do sleuthing and have quite a reputation for being good at it. Is it the Alpines? I mean, they are the only ones invested in Natasha's disqualification." She worried her bottom lip with her teeth. "I wish now we'd never disqualified her. She wouldn't have won anyway because Julie had her beat in score, but what if we hadn't done it? Would Winona and Patricia still be alive?" Tears came to her eyes.

"There's no telling," I said. "Right now, we have no proof who the killer or killers are. It's why it's important that you not be alone."

Tears ran down her cheeks. She grabbed a tissue and dabbed at her face. "Winona was my friend. We worked together on all the same committees and I worked as her assistant. Now that she's gone, I don't know what I'm going to do."

I squeezed her hand. "I'm sure you'll find a new job.

You are highly qualified, and everyone knows how much you helped Winona."

She shook her head and grabbed a second tissue and blew her nose. "All I can do is step up and take her place on the committees for now. But it was all volunteer work. I just feel lost and now I'm in danger. Maybe I should move to Chicago."

"I can't tell you what to do," I said, "but I've heard the best thing to do when you have such a loss is to not make any big decisions for a few months. Why don't you call your mom? I've got to go, but if you ever feel unsafe, please call Rex. If you feel lonely, come by the McMurphy. I've always got time to make tea and comfort a friend."

"Thanks, Allie," she said and stood. "I just might take you up on that."

I gave her a quick hug. "Take care, Michelle, and I'll see you at the committee meeting."

"Bye, Allie." She walked me out. I stepped out and was again caught by the beauty of her yard. "Who does your gardening? This yard is gorgeous."

She blushed. "Thanks, I do it myself. My mother is a master gardener and taught me everything I know."

"Well, it's so nice."

"Thanks again," she said. I stepped off the porch and noticed Charles bike by. He stopped and got off his bike.

"Allie," he said.

"Hi, Charles," I said. "She seems fine."

"I'm going to have a look around anyway," he said. "Best to be safe."

I left Michelle satisfied she'd be all right. As all right as the rest of us, anyway.

Chapter 17

"Allie, welcome, what brings you to the Chamber of Commerce?" Florence Bluebird, the tourism bureau chief, greeted me with a quick hug. Florence was tall and thin with long black hair and coppery skin. Her brown eyes were warm and welcoming. Dressed in a pencil skirt and white shirt, she was the very picture of business cool.

"I have a question," I said.

"Well, come on in and have a seat. We're always ready to help a chamber member. Can I get you some water or tea?"

"No, thanks," I said and sat down on the comfy chair across from her desk. The office was small, but well kept. "I was wondering if you could tell me if Winona Higer and Patricia Ramsfeld were working on anything other than the Midsummer Night's Festival."

"Oh, yes, poor Winona and Patricia. That was a terrible thing to happen to them. Are you investigating their murder?"

"I'm trying to keep my friend Carol Tunisian safe," I hedged. "I was wondering if the murders had anything to do with a project they might be working on."

"Well, they both were regular volunteers for projects, but as far as I understand, they were not connected to anything for the chamber."

"That's certainly a relief." I sat back in the chair.

"How is the McMurphy doing? I know you had a lot of work done to the old girl. Are you happy with the outcome?"

"Yes, I think she's better than ever," I said. "With Jenn running an event planning business out of her, we're seeing higher-than-ever stay rates."

"Wonderful! I love seeing more people coming and enjoying all that Mackinac Island has to offer. What kind of events have you hosted so far?"

"Weddings, a fiftieth-anniversary family party, and we are bidding for the high school reunion cocktail parties."

"But the reunions are quite small, and most people have relatives still living here, so why bid on the reunion?"

"Jenn thought it would be a way to get the locals to visit our rooftop desk and see what the McMurphy has to offer when they have guests staying," I said.

"Okay, interesting," she said. "We do have a golf tournament scheduled this year. Perhaps you would consider sponsoring a hole?"

"Sure, I'd consider it," I said. "Any information you can give me will help." She handed me a pamphlet and walked me to the door.

"I certainly urge you to consider a sponsorship. It's great publicity for the McMurphy."

"I will," I said. "Thanks for your time." I walked out without any information that might actually help solve the murder, but I did have a chance to sponsor a hole in the tournament. That was until I saw how much it cost. Better to offer a two-night stay and a pound of fudge.

Chapter 18

"The Chamber of Commerce was a bust," I said to Frances. "As far as Florence knew, the two ladies weren't working on any projects for them. Oh, and she was hoping we'd sponsor a hole in the golf tournament, but it's way above our budget."

Jenn came down the stairs. "There's a golf tournament?"

"The Chamber of Commerce is sponsoring it," I said and handed her the pamphlet. "Florence wanted us to sponsor a hole, but it's way out of my league. We can do a two-night stay and a pound of fudge for the silent auction, though."

"It might be worth it for the PR," Jenn said. "I could offer a wedding carriage ride. Or we could offer a cocktail party on the roof."

"We don't have a liquor license," I reminded her. "It would have to be BYOB."

"Okay, carriage ride it is," she said. "Do you want me to tell Florence?"

"Sure," I said and glanced at my phone. "They're closed right now, so you'll need to schedule your call tomorrow. Frances, are all our guests checked in?"

"They are," she said.

"Well, it's after five. Why don't we all go up for a drink like we used to?"

"Oh, we're sorry, but we have plans," Frances said and looked at Douglas, who nodded.

"I can't either," Jenn said. "I'm meeting Shane for dinner before he has to go back to work. With two murders he's working extra-long hours."

"I get it," I said and picked up Mal. "Rex is working overtime, too. It was a thought."

"We'll take a rain check," Frances said.

"Rain check it is," I agreed. "Have a good night." I watched them grab their light jackets and walk out the door together. Times certainly were changing. "Come on, Mal, let's go get Mella and you some dinner."

I decided to use the time to experiment with new flavors of fudge. Small batches in my kitchen were the best way to experiment. This time I was working on more sophisticated flavors like cardamom and chai, green tea and lemon. As I worked away tweaking the recipes, I got a call from Suzanne McGee.

"Hi, Allie," she said. "I'm on the decoration committee for Main Street and we were wondering if you would like to be a part of our committee."

"The decoration committee?"

"Yes, we take care of putting up the potted flowers, the Fourth of July banners, the fall decorations, and the Christmas decorations."

"Oh, of course," I said. "There's a pole right outside the McMurphy."

"Yes, you see Patricia was a member of the committee and, with her passing, we have a hole to fill. You were our first choice. Mrs. Tunisian told us you were looking to be involved in the community . . ."

"Yes," I said. "Of course, you can count on me."

"Wonderful," she said. "We have a committee meeting the first Wednesday of every month at seven p.m."

"Okay." I wrote that down. "So, two weeks from today?"

"No, we're calling a special meeting tomorrow afternoon at four. Please come to the community room at Pierre's Bed-and-Breakfast. We'll have tea service and introductions."

"Got it," I said. "I'll see you then."

"Thanks, Allie," Suzanne said. "See you then. Ta-ta." She hung up and I poured my pets their dinners and fed them. The decoration committee. I wonder if Patricia's killer might have known her from that.

I poured myself a glass of wine and grabbed my favorite cozy mystery and sat down to read. Mella finished her dinner and jumped up to rest on the top of my chair near my ear. Mal jumped up in my lap and we settled in for a quiet night until there was a knock at my door.

Mal rushed to the door, barking. I got up and looked outside the peephole that I'd had placed in both of my doors. The knock had come from the back staircase and it was Rex standing there. I opened the door.

"Hi," I said and noted the misty rain that had started to fall. "Come on in before you get soaked." He stepped in and took off his hat, wiping his feet on the rug by the door and then taking off his shoes. "I brought dinner. I hope you don't mind."

"No, of course not," I said and took the bags from him.

"It's Chinese from the buffet in Mackinaw City. I hope it's not too cold," he said and shook off his coat and walked to the coatrack to hang it.

"The best part about Chinese food is that it's easy to reheat," I said. I took out some soup and put it in a big bowl and heated it up. "Can I get you a beer or wine?"

"A beer would be great," he said and rubbed his hands over his face.

"You look exhausted," I said as I handed him an opened bottle. "You were on the lower peninsula?"

"I was talking to Patricia's niece and her family about who might have done this to her."

"And did they know?" I asked as I took the egg drop soup out of the microwave and served it up in two bowls. The egg rolls took only a minute in the microwave and then sesame chicken was just as quick.

I pulled up a barstool and dipped my spoon into the soup. It was hot and rich.

"They haven't got a clue," he said. "It's the same with Winona's family. Everyone says no one would have had a reason to even be mad at the two, let alone kill them."

"I know we were thinking they were related to the pageant," I said. "But I've been thinking. Are women more likely to kill using a gun?"

"I know plenty of women who like to hunt, so yeah, I think a rifle would be handy to most anyone on the island."

"Were they killed by a rifle?"

He shook his head. "The evidence says it was a pistol, which I believe because someone would have noticed a person carrying a rifle to the bonfire. A handgun can be easier to conceal."

"Well, I suppose a woman could carry a handgun"—I waved my soup spoon—"but it seems like she would find a less bloody way of killing."

"Typically," he said as he chewed on an egg roll. "But we can't rule women out."

"So, you do think the Alpines are still involved somehow?"

"I didn't say that," he said. "The note that Carol got might have been written by a woman, but I can't tie it to the two murders."

"Two murders in three days," I said. "It has to be worrisome."

"It is," he said. "Let's change the subject. Anything new happen in your day?"

"I was asked to be a member of the Main Street decoration committee," I said. "We meet tomorrow for tea and a meet and greet."

"Interesting," he said. "Why all of a sudden?"

"Patricia was a member, and they were looking for her replacement," I said. "Feels kind of sudden since she isn't even out of the morgue yet."

"Suzanne always was on the ball," he said. "She had my mom on a committee within two hours of one of the elderly member's death."

"That was fast."

He shook his head. "The woman gets things done."

"Which means by this time tomorrow, I'll have more work to do," I said.

"And you'll leave the investigating to me, right?"

"Don't I always?" I said as innocently as possible.

He sent me a look and I ate a piece of chicken.

Chapter 19

The next afternoon, I walked out of my apartment dressed in a sundress and sweater with dressy sandals.

"Where are you off to looking so cute?" Jenn asked when I passed by the office door.

"I've got a welcome tea for the decoration committee," I said, sticking my head into the office. "How was the Westminsters' wedding?"

"A complete success, if I don't say so myself." Jenn grinned. "The customer satisfaction surveys went out and people are giving us rave reviews."

"Wonderful! What's up next?"

"The Nelson wedding on Friday and the Parrishes' twenty-fifth anniversary on Saturday," she said. "Jim and Helen Parrish were married on the island and wanted to bring their children and parents here to celebrate. They've got the whole third floor and we're catering the dinner on the rooftop on Saturday night."

"Sounds great! Hopefully it won't rain."

"We have the white tent if it does," she said. "They just miss the great views of the straits. I put both events on your calendar. Which, by the way, is getting really busy."

Jenn usually brought in a caterer for these events, but she always liked me to be there to welcome the guests to the McMurphy. "I agree," I said, "but the festival committee has its last meeting this week, then nothing until January when we start to plan next year's festival. I'm going to push for not having a pageant. I think it would be fine without one."

"Pageants were Winona's thing," she said. "I'm sure no one will disagree."

I glanced at my phone. "Oh, boy, I've got to go if I don't want to be late."

"See you!"

I hurried down the stairs and patted Mal on the head before waving goodbye to Frances and heading out. It was a gorgeous afternoon in the low seventies with bright sunlight and the scent of fudge, popcorn, and flowers in the air. I avoided a horse and carriage carrying tourists and headed for the admin building.

Walking into the auditorium, I saw a long table filled with tea cakes, cookies, small sandwiches, and pots of hot water and selections of tea, milk, and honey. Suzanne met me near the door. "Allie, come on in, I'm so glad you joined us." She put her arm through mine and walked me down to where ten other people gathered. She made introductions. I knew most of them from the town hall meetings the mayor put on. I picked up a cup and saucer and made myself a cup of green tea.

"Allie, are you on this committee now?" Mayor Boatman asked as she met me at the table and moved to pick up a teacup.

"Yes," I said and snagged a cookie.

"It makes sense with the McMurphy on Main Street." She leaned in toward me. "I have to ask: Are you investigating our latest string of murders?"

"Right now, I'm getting to know the people on the committee better," I hedged.

"Oh," the mayor said. "Right. Well, it's just that I have a theory."

"You do?" My ears perked up.

"Yes. You see, both Winona and Patricia were in the community sewing circle," she said, leaning in close. "Everyone knows the sewing circle is a hotbed of emotion. If you know what I mean."

"No," I said, confused.

"It's easy to get on the wrong side of somebody and start a feud."

"You think Winona and Patricia were on the wrong side?" I suggested.

"Exactly," she said and straightened. "Now go do what you do—ah, Brittany, so nice to see you." She turned to Brittany Zell and just like that, I was dismissed.

Still, I had a lead. I didn't know what went on at this infamous sewing circle, but I sure knew people who would know.

Chapter 20

Amy met me at five in the lobby of the McMurphy. She wore a black T-shirt and black pants. "Allie," she said. "I didn't know what to wear for a stakeout, but I thought, black? We're not going to be in a car to hide in."

I was still dressed in a sundress. "Anything would be fine," I said. "We just need to blend into the crowds."

"Well, we'd better hurry. Rick left for the stables fifteen minutes ago."

"Got it," I said. "Just a second." I stuck my head into the fudge shop. "Need anything before I run out?"

"No, I'm good," Madison said. She was working out just fine. She had quickly picked up how to help with the fudge demonstrations and working the cash register was easy for her. Frances had picked a real winner.

"Okay, let's go," I said, grabbed Mal and her leash and clipped it on.

"You're bringing your dog?" Amy asked, her forehead wrinkled with worry.

"Mal's the perfect cover," I said. "If anyone asks what we're doing, we're just walking my dog. Besides, we can drink our coffee outside the Lucky Bean and keep an eye on the stables."

"Huh," she said. "You are brilliant."

We hurried out and down Main Street, dodging the crowds. Mal loved the crowds, but I liked that Wednesdays were less busy than the weekends. We turned down Hoban Street, then back up Market. This allowed us to pass the stables and peer inside.

"There's Rick," Amy whispered, and we hurried past before he could look up and see us.

"Good, then we'll have a good view from the Lucky Bean," I said.

I snagged a bistro table outside the coffee shop and Amy went in to get us drinks.

"Allie?"

It was Carol and Irma Gooseman. They came power walking my way.

"Ladies," I said. "How are you? Carol, it's good to see you out and I'm glad you aren't alone."

"Staying safe," Carol said, as they stopped to sit with me.

Amy came out with our drinks. "Oh, hi, ladies," she said and handed me my coffee. "How are you?"

"We're good," Carol said. She handed Irma cash. "Can you bring me a latte?" Irma got up and went inside to get their drinks. "What brings you ladies out here this time of day?"

Amy blushed. "No reason," she hedged.

"We're doing some sleuthing," I said. "But trying to blend in, so having you ladies stop and sit with us is a good thing." I said this to Amy, so she'd relax.

"What are you sleuthing?" Irma asked as she came out with two lattes and took a seat.

"Mayor Boatman told me that Winona and Patricia were in the sewing circle," I said. "And we're out seeing if we can run into other members of the circle. Amy knows one of them," I covered.

"That's right," Amy said. "Debbie Moore. She sometimes comes by this way after work."

"Ah," Carol said. "I didn't think about the sewing circle."

"I think the mayor may be onto something," Irma said. "Just last night, Irene was telling me that Winona had been helping with a new quilt."

"That doesn't sound like anything to kill for," I pointed out.

"Then you don't know sewing circles," Carol said. "You see, there's been a tussle for years over who was going to lead the circle."

"That's right," Irma said and nodded her head. "In fact, Winona and Patricia have been at each other's throats about the quilt style for years. Each one vies for their design to be the next one. It was a whole thing until Mary Emry decided to put all the names in a hat and draw out who got to pick the next design."

"Wow," Carol said as she wiggled in her chair, her hands wrapped around a half-full mug of coffee. "That's why the two were so cold to each other on the festival committee. I wondered what that was about."

"Do you think that Patricia killed Winona and then herself?" Irma asked, her big blue eyes serious.

"I don't think that Patricia could have killed herself," I said. "There wasn't a gun at the scene."

"Wait, so Patricia was shot, too?" Irma's eyes lit up.

"I didn't say that," I hedged.

"Maybe they just didn't find the murder weapon," Carol said. "We should go back and look."

"Maybe tomorrow," I said. "Right now, we're sleuthing."

"Fine," Carol said with a big smile. "We'll see you at eleven after your fudge demonstration." She stood. "I'm excited. Maybe we should go without you."

"I don't think you should," I said. "There's safety in numbers. Please wait until tomorrow."

"All right." Irma stood. "Come on, Carol, we need to finish our power walk." The ladies tossed their cups in the trash and power walked away.

"That was close," Amy said. "Thanks for covering."

"You didn't seem like you wanted anyone to know what we were doing and so I figured a partial lie was best." A movement from the stables caught my eye. It was Rick. "He's leaving already?"

Amy turned to see him going away from us on Market Street. "I knew he couldn't have that much overtime work at the stables." She teared up. "Can we follow him?"

"Certainly," I said. We followed him down to Pumpkin Jack's stables, where he went inside. Amy and I continued down Cadotte Street, walking Mal. "Well, he's not doing anything untoward," I pointed out.

"Not yet," she said.

"Why are you so sure he's cheating?"

"He's been preoccupied." She paced while Mal sniffed the bushes. "A wife knows when something's going on."

"When does he usually get home?"

"Around nine," she said.

"We can wait out here until then, if you want," I said. "Then we'll see if he goes anywhere else."

"Do you mind?"

"Not at all," I said. "Mal loves long walks and the weather is wonderful. Let's walk around the block."

We walked around the block at least five times before we spotted Rick coming out of Pumpkin Jack's and this time, instead of turning toward home, he went down Lake Shore Drive. We followed at a distance until we saw him cut off the road to a path that led up to a cabin.

"What's he doing there?" Amy whispered. We hung out behind a tree and watched around the corner.

A woman opened the door, and he wiped his feet, then went inside. I glanced at my phone: It was seven p.m. "Maybe he's doing work for her?"

"Or maybe he's having an affair," Amy said. "I'm going to go up and knock on the door and demand he give me some answers."

"Are you sure?" I asked. "Because I think it's best if I come by tomorrow and see what the woman has to say."

"You'd ask her for me? What if she lies? No, I think it's best if I confront them right now."

"Why don't we wait?" I suggested and grabbed her arm to hold her back. "He hasn't been there long enough to do anything. What if he leaves?"

"Fine," she said. "But if he's not out of there in thirty minutes, I'm going in."

"I guess that's fair," I said. "Come on, Let's walk a ways down Lake Shore and get some of that angry energy out. Keep in mind, this could all be innocent. Besides, she looked older."

"That doesn't mean anything," Amy said. "Men have

affairs with older women just as much as younger women."

We headed down Lake Shore Drive and got five minutes away when Amy stopped. "No—you know what, I'm going to go home." She had tears in her eyes. "I'll confront him at home."

"Are you sure?"

"I'm sure," she said. "My stomach is sick, and I just want to go home."

"Okay," I said. "I'll walk you there."

"Thanks," she said. "Thanks for doing this with me. It's been a few hours out of your day and I really appreciate it."

"No problem," I said. I walked her home and left her at her door. It was growing dark out and Mal and I hurried down the street. I thought I heard footsteps behind me. I turned to look, but no one was there. "Come on, Mal," I said. "Let's jog." I took off running, fully aware that I was alone for the first time since Carol showed me the threatening letter. I didn't think I was on the killer's list of committee members, but it was best to get home safely anyway.

One thing I had learned is you just never knew for sure what was going on in other people's minds.

Cinnamon Mocha Fudge

Ingredients:
3 cups of semisweet chocolate chips
1 14-ounce can of sweetened condensed milk
2 tablespoons of strong brewed coffee
1 teaspoon cinnamon
dash of salt
1 teaspoon of vanilla

Directions
Line an 8x8-inch pan with buttered parchment paper. In a microwave safe bowl mix chocolate chips, sweetened condensed milk, coffee, cinnamon, and salt. Microwave on high for 30 seconds, stir and repeat until chocolate mixture is almost smooth. It will continue to melt after you remove it from the microwave. Stir in vanilla and pour into pan. Cool and cut into one-inch squares. Makes two pounds. Enjoy!

Chapter 21

Carol and Irma showed up at eleven on the dot the next morning.

"Allie," Carol said. "Are you ready to check out the crime scene?" Carol's eyes glittered with glee. "We'll use flashlights like they do on the crime shows."

"It's the middle of the morning," I said as I took off my hat and chef coat. "You won't need flashlights."

"We can still use them," she said. "You never know what shadows are hiding. Maybe we should get a blue light and look for blood."

"I think that's gruesome and over the top," I said as I hung up my gear.

"Well, you stay here then and we'll go." Carol was wearing a sweatshirt and blue polyester pants and produced a small flashlight out of her pants pocket.

"I've got one, too." Irma pulled hers out of the pocket of her sweater.

"Seriously, it's daylight. What are you doing with flashlights?" I asked.

"If we want to stay until dark then we need to have a way to see ourselves home," Carol said.

"We have streetlights," I pointed out. "Besides, that's hours away and you shouldn't be out after dark."

"Spoilsport," Carol said. "Are you coming or not?"

"I'm coming," I said. "I need to change first. Why don't you two come up to my apartment and have a cup of coffee while I change."

"Okay," Irma said as they followed me up the stairs. "But you won't be able to distract us from our mission."

"Trust me, I won't," I said. "Somebody's got to look out for you two."

Fifteen minutes later we were walking down Main Street toward the school. Mal led the way, sniffing the ground. It was as if she knew where we were going. The crime scene tape was gone, and you wouldn't have known anything happened in the area.

"This is the spot," I said. "Mal found her in the bushes right here." I pointed out the lilac bush.

"Was she face up or face down?" Carol asked.

"Face down," I said.

"So, she could have stood here," Carol said, planting her feet in front of the bush. "And shot herself in the head."

"Are we still going with the murder-suicide theory? If she shot herself in the head, then she wouldn't fall forward," I said. "Don't you think the momentum of the gun would throw her back into the street?"

Carol mimed the action. "I think you're right." She turned on her flashlight and we walked around the back of the bush. "She would have stood about here." Carol put Irma in the spot, formed her hand as a gun, and mimicked shooting Irma in the head. "She would have fallen into the bushes . . . face up." Carol and Irma frowned.

"If she were shot, she must have been facing the bush," I said. "Why would she be facing the bush?"

"Maybe she was spying on someone," Irma said. "They found her and shot her."

"Who would she be spying on?" I asked.

Irma acted like she was spying, and Carol went around and pretended to shoot her.

"It just doesn't work," Carol said. "She would have landed face down this way. And you said she was face down that way."

"She must have been moved," I said and tapped my chin.

"By whom and why?" Irma asked.

"The killer, of course," Carol said.

"Of all the places to hide a body, why a bush just off Lake Shore Drive where people walk by on a regular basis?" I asked.

"Unless the body was too heavy and the killer could only take it so far," Carol said.

"Someone could have been coming and they panicked and shoved her in the bush," Irma reasoned. "You found her, right?"

"Yes," I said.

"Maybe they saw you coming and shoved her in the bush and ran," Irma said.

"Now that could be," I said. "Then, where's the crime

scene if it's not here?" I glanced around in a 360 circle. "There's not a lot of ground cover here. She had to be shot nearby and dragged here." I looked for drag marks, walking a careful circle around the bushes. "Here!" I pointed to two faint marks in the grass. The ladies hurried toward me.

"That looks like drag marks to me," Carol said.

I followed the marks as far as I could to a spot near the sidewalk on the front of the school. "The drag marks stop here." I glanced around. "With school out for the season, this is a relatively hidden area. Patricia must have been walking along the sidewalk, met the killer, and BANG!"

Carol put Irma in the spot and pretended to shoot her. Irma went down and then Carol tried to lift her under the arms and drag her. "This is hard work," Carol said. "Not sure a senior citizen could pull this off."

"Maybe Irene could," Irma said. "She's always at the gym working with the weight machines."

I searched the area and found a shell casing. I took out my phone and took a picture of it. Then grabbed a pen out of my pocket and picked it up, careful not to touch it. We all studied it, the two older women flashing their flashlights at it. "I need to take this to Rex," I said.

"We'll go with you," Irma said. "We can be your witnesses that you found the shell here."

"I think three of us might be a little too much," I said. "I'll catch you two tomorrow."

"Okay," Carol said. "I guess we know when we've outstayed our welcome. Wouldn't want to get between you lovebirds."

I shook my head and headed to the police department. I met Charles on the way out when I was on the way in.

"Oh, Allie," he said. "How are you?"

"I'm well," I said. "I may have found some evidence from Patricia's shooting."

"How? Why?" He looked concerned.

I lifted the pen with the shell casing on it. "I found this near the school and thought it might be related to Patricia's murder."

Charles pulled an evidence bag out of his pocket. "Let's put that in here." He opened the bag and I put the shell inside. "Shane will be mad that you found it and he missed it."

We walked into the police building together and Charles took me back to where Rex worked at his desk. "Hey, Rex," he said. "Allie found a shell casing."

"What?" Rex looked up.

Charles lifted the evidence bag. "She found a shell casing near the school."

"What were you doing out near the school?" Rex asked. His face was filled with concern.

"Mrs. Tunisian and Mrs. Gooseman wanted to go out to see if they could prove that Patricia killed herself," I explained. "I didn't want them to go out alone."

"That was a good idea," he said, "especially since Mrs. Tunisian found that threatening note."

"How did you find the shell?" Charles asked as he handed the evidence bag to Rex. "Shane went over the scene with a fine-tooth comb."

"We followed the drag marks," I said.

"You found drag marks," Rex said suspiciously.

"We did," I said. "I'm sure Shane did too."

"He did," Rex said. "We knew she was dumped in the bush. But we didn't find any shell casings."

"Maybe the lighting was right," I said. "I saw a glint in the grass and picked it up. But I took a picture of it first." I showed him the photo on my phone. "I thought that way you could connect it to the crime scene."

"Good work," Charles said.

"Shane will be upset," Rex said. "You know you're making him look bad."

"Anyone could have missed it," I said.

"Right," Rex said. "It's better if you leave these things to the pros."

"I know," I said. "But I'm also not going to let those two old ladies go out and get themselves in trouble."

"Okay, then," Charles said. "I'll let you two hash this out. Have a good day, Allie."

"Bye," Rex and I said at the same time. Rex put the shell on his desk, and I sat down beside him.

"I'm not trying to make anyone look bad," I said. "You know that, right?"

"I'm not offended, Allie," he said. "I'm saying Shane might be. Truth is, I'm just worried about you out chasing a killer who has already murdered twice."

"I don't think I'm in any danger," I said.

"But you are investigating," he said.

"I haven't found anything important enough to tell you about," I said.

"Why did the ladies think Patricia might have killed herself?"

"There was some sort of rivalry in the sewing circle between Patricia and Winona and the ladies thought that it might have been a murder-suicide."

"Hard to kill yourself and throw away the gun," Rex said.

"Yes, well, we had to go through the motions." I shrugged. "Are you working late?"

"Yeah, I've got two murders' worth of paperwork to do," he said.

"Then I'll leave you to it." I stood, kissed him, and walked out. Mal was happy to leave and go back to her Scooby-Doo sniffing. Luckily, we didn't find any more bodies on our way back home. I went up the back stairs to my apartment and opened the door. Mella met us and snuck out. I let her; she often went out to visit Shelia and I respected her ability to do so. If I had it my way, she would be a house cat, but Mella had her own mind and liked to check out her territory and visit her old owner.

"Come on, Mal," I said. My pup wanted to go with Mella. "Let's get back to work." I closed and locked my door behind me. My thoughts were on the shell casing I'd found. I didn't know much about guns, so I went to my computer and did a quick search. It seemed automatic handguns shot out casings, but revolvers didn't. This meant that Rex would know what type of gun and not have to worry about ballistics, at least for Patricia.

They still had to connect the two murders. Rex didn't seem to be in any hurry to do so. I guess I, too, had to consider two murderers with the same MO.

Chapter 22

Later that afternoon Roni Clark stopped into the McMurphy. I'd just finished my last fudge demonstration. "Hi Allie," she said. "Suzanne told me to stop in and ask if you'd help me with the hanging flowerpots."

I stepped out of the fudge shop and walked with Roni through the lobby. Roni was in her mid-thirties and was a fifth-generation Mackinac Islander. She had short brown hair and wide green eyes and wore jeans and a plaid shirt.

"The flowerpots on the Main Street decoration poles?" I asked to clarify.

"Yes," Roni said. "I'm going on vacation for two weeks and was wondering if you'd take over watering them?"

"Sure, why not?" I said.

"Great! All you have to do is water them once a week.

I usually water on Fridays and give them a good drink," she said.

"Do you use a watering can?"

"No," she said. "A hose will do; you just have to use some of the store's outdoor spigots." She reached into her pocket. "I drew up a map of all the places you can attach a hose and water the plants. I try and do it early because you don't want to be doing it when the fudgies come in off the ferries."

I took the map from her and studied it. "Are you sure it's okay?"

"Absolutely," she said. "I need you to start this week and next, as I'm off on vacation in about two hours."

"Well, you can count on me," I said.

She smiled. "That's what Suzanne said. Thank you!" She headed toward the door.

"Have a good vacation," I called after her.

"What was that all about?" Frances asked me.

"I got my first duty assignment for the decoration committee. Looks like I'll be out watering the flowers tomorrow morning."

"Well, that's not too bad," Frances said.

"Let's hope not," I said. I went upstairs to get out of my fudge making clothes when there was a knock on my back door. Mal barked and raced to the door. I looked out the peephole to see Amy standing there. I opened the door. "Amy—"

She pushed into my apartment. "I couldn't do it. I couldn't talk to him about her."

"Well, I guess I understand that," I said. "It's tough to have hard conversations."

"I want to confront her." Amy paced in front of my bar. "I asked around and her name is Ashley Barington.

She's married to Thomas Barington and the shame of it is that they have two children."

"What are you going to do? Go knock on her door?"

"Yes," Amy said. "Would you go with me?"

"Well, I—"

"Please," she said. "I'm going either way, but it would be nice to have someone there who also saw Rick go into her home."

"Fine," I said. "Let me change really quick." I climbed out of my fudge making clothes and into a sundress. Then I texted Frances that I was on an errand and asked if she needed me to pick up anything for her.

She texted back that she was okay.

I put Mal on her leash and Amy and I went out the back door and down the steps to the alley. "Are you sure you want to do this?" I asked. "It's kind of a big thing."

"I want to see her face when I tell her what we saw. I figure she'll give away her shock at being caught. Then I'd like to punch her in the nose."

"I don't think punching her is a good choice," I said. "I can't condone it. She could charge you with assault."

"Fine," Amy said as she strode quickly down Market Street toward Lake Shore Drive. "Then I'll just tell her to keep her hands off my man."

"I guess that's reasonable," I said. I thought of Melonic, Rex's second wife, and her anger at me for dating Rex. Would she have punched me in the face? Somehow, I thought she might.

We cut off the road and up the path to the house where we'd seen Rick knock on the door and be let in. The home was a log cabin, and it was beautifully made. Amy built up a good head of steam and Mal and I had to be on our toes to stay caught up to her.

"Slow down and take a breath," I said.

"I've got to do this before I change my mind," she replied and banged on the door. I could hear someone coming through the house when Amy banged again. "Hello?"

The door opened and a lovely woman of about forty answered. She had her hair up in a messy bun and looked like she'd been doing yoga. My heart went into my throat.

"Ashley Barington?" Amy asked.

"Yes, can I help you?"

"Yes, you can start by keeping your hands off my husband!" Amy shouted.

"What?" Ashley looked confused. "Who? I'm a married woman."

"Exactly and you should be ashamed, having an affair with my husband, Rick. Don't lie about it. We followed him last night and saw him come here from the stables. You let him in."

"Your husband is Rick Houseman?" she asked.

"Yes," Amy said with tears in her eyes. "And you should know that I won't take his affair lying down."

"Oh, honey, we're not having an affair," Ashley said.

That took the wind out of Amy's sails. "You're not? Then why is he coming here at night and telling me that he's working late at the stables?"

"Rick is doing a wrought iron art piece I commissioned for my husband for our anniversary," Ashley said. "Please come in. Let me get you some iced tea. I'll show you the art piece. It's in the basement."

"Why wouldn't he tell me about it?" Amy asked.

"Yes, it does seem odd," I said as we entered the beautiful home. The kitchen was huge, with skylights and large windows to let in the sun. She motioned for us to sit down at the kitchen table and proceeded to get us iced teas.

"I asked him not to tell a soul," Ashley said. "You know how small-town Mackinac Island is. I thought if anyone knew—even you, Mrs. Houseman—then word would get out to my Thomas. You see, he works down at the docks as a fishing guide. He hears everything that happens on the island before I do." She handed us each a tall glass of iced tea and sat down beside me. "It was just a precautionary measure. I had no idea you would think Rick and I were having an affair. What led you to that conclusion?"

"The secrecy," Amy said and took a gulp of tea to calm herself. "He refused to tell me anything other than he was working overtime at the stables. It just didn't sound right."

"She asked me to do some sleuthing with her," I said and Mal climbed into my lap. "We followed Rick here last night."

"I almost confronted you then," Amy said. "But my heart wouldn't let me." She put her hand on her heart. "Oh, the fear and anger I felt. I barely slept."

"I can understand that," Ashley said. "I don't know what I'd do if I thought my Thomas was keeping secrets from me." She sent Amy a soft smile. "Your husband is a pure gentleman and very much in love with you. He would never step out like that."

"Can we see the art?" I asked.

"Certainly." She stood. I put Mal down and we followed her to the basement door. She opened it and turned on the light and led us down the stairs. "I know it seems odd to hide the art in the basement, but it's where I do laundry and Thomas doesn't come down here. It's sort of my she shed, if I have one."

Downstairs was light and bright. There were shelves filled with quilting scraps and yarn balls. A sewing machine was front and center along with the washer and dryer and a lovely laundry folding table.

"It's around the corner in the storage room," she said. She opened a door and clicked on a light. There was a lovely wrought iron fisherman. "It's almost done."

"It's beautiful," I said. "Amy, I didn't know Rick was such an artist."

"I did," Amy said. "He went to fine art school and studied metals and sculpting. It doesn't pay well so he became a blacksmith and farrier part-time."

"This is amazing," I went on. "I think we should have the town commission some pieces for Main Street. I know I'd love one right outside the McMurphy."

"That's a wonderful idea," Ashley said. "I'm on a first-name basis with the mayor. It's a great idea for the downtown beautification committee."

"Wow, if he was commissioned to sculpt, he could have his own studio just like he's always dreamed," Amy said. "Who would have thought I came here to wrongfully accuse you and you would put in a good word for him. Thank you."

"My pleasure," she said, and we left the closet and went back upstairs. "I'm so glad you stopped by. I'm afraid if you had gone to Rick with this, he would have felt compelled to keep my secret. That would have just made things worse."

"Yes, it would have," Amy said. "Well, we won't keep you."

"I do have a quick question," I said. "I saw that you sew."

"I quilt, actually. I make quilts for cancer patients."

"Of course, you do," Amy said wryly.

"Do you by chance belong to the sewing circle?" I picked Mal up.

"I do, why?" Ashley asked.

"I understand that Winona and Patricia both belonged to the circle. Would you know if there was any bad blood between them and anyone else?"

"You mean, would someone from the sewing circle want to kill them?" Ashley asked. "I can imagine that someone would. Those two ladies were always at odds with each other and then other ladies in the circle. I swear they made someone angry every other week. So, yes, I can imagine the killer is from the sewing circle. The thing is that this has been going on for years. So why kill now?"

"Maybe the killer had reached a breaking point and just snapped," I suggested. "Is there anyone you think might fit that bill?"

"I can think of one or two," Ashley said. She grabbed a piece of paper and a pen and wrote something down and handed it to me. "Go see Blanche Snodgrass. Here's her address. If anyone in the sewing circle was plotting murder, Blanche would be the one to know."

"Thanks," I said as we stepped out onto the back deck.

"Just one thing," Ashley said. "Don't tell her I sent you. I don't want to be embroiled in anything. Okay?"

"Okay," I agreed. No embroiling her in any dispute, especially murder.

Chapter 23

The next morning, I'd finished filling the counter with fudge and had put on a light jacket and taken Mal out for her morning walk. We were up the street, close to the senior center, when I heard my name being called.

"Allie, thank goodness you're here," Carol said as she stormed my way. "You have to come to my house."

"What's going on?" I asked.

"Irma and I just got back from our power walk and someone's broken into my home."

"Oh, that's not good," I said and Mal and I hurried to Carol's house. She opened her picket fence and took us around the two track and grass drive to the back door.

"See?"

The window in the door was smashed and the door was standing open. "Have you gone in?"

"No," Carol said. "I guess I panicked and went down the street to get the police when I saw you."

"I'll call Rex," I said and got out my phone. "Don't touch anything." I dialed Rex's number.

"Manning," he answered, his voice sexy gruff.

"Rex, it's Allie," I said. "I'm with Carol and someone's broken into her home."

"Are you safe?" he asked, his voice changing to all business.

I glanced around. "I think so. We're outside and the back door is smashed and open."

"Go around to the front and stay out of the house," he said. "I'm on my way."

We went out to the front porch and sat down on the porch swing until Rex arrived and kickstanded his bike. "Are you ladies okay?"

"We're fine," I said. "We've been sitting here waiting for you."

"Stay here," he said and went around the back.

We stood and peered our heads around the corner and watched as he disappeared.

"Who could have done such a thing?" Carol said. "I've lived on the island my whole life and never had anyone break in. This is so shocking."

I put my arm around her. "It's going to be okay."

"I wish my husband were here," she said. "He's on a month long fishing trip in Canada."

"Gosh, so you're really home alone?"

"Yes," she said with tears in her eyes.

I gave her a squeeze and the front door opened. Rex stuck his head out.

"It's safe, you ladies can come inside."

We went in through the front and the living room was pristine.

"Looks like they didn't get to the living room," I said.

"I think you came home before they thought you would," Rex said as we moved into the kitchen. The kitchen was a torn-up mess. There were dishes everywhere, flour and sugar strewn across the floor, on the cabinets and on the table. Written in the flour were the words *you're next*. I felt a shiver run down my spine.

"How could they have left without me seeing them?" Carol asked. "I was here, saw the door and went straight to find help."

"You left to find help," I said. "They could have gotten away then."

"True," Carol mused.

"The kitchen wasn't the only room they tore apart," Rex said. "They were also in your bedroom." We followed Carol through the kitchen door to the back bedroom and saw that it too was tossed. Her mattress was flipped; sheets and blankets everywhere. Carol put her hand to her mouth and made a small sound.

I put my hand on her shoulder. "It's going to be all right," I said. "I'll help you right it."

"They were in my bedroom." She moved as if to pick up the underwear scattered on the floor.

"Don't touch anything," Rex said. "I've called in Shane. He needs to go over the house for evidence. You don't make this kind of mess without leaving evidence."

"Who would want to do this?" Carol asked.

"Who knew what time you went power walking every morning?" Rex asked and took a pen and small pad of paper out of his pocket.

"I guess anyone could have known," Carol said. "Irma and I go every day and we see a lot of people on our walk."

"*Anyone* is not helpful," Rex muttered. "You go at the exact same time daily?"

"At my age you become a creature of habit," Carol said. "Besides, it's Mackinac Island. It's safe."

"Not currently," I said.

"Any idea why you would be targeted?" Rex asked.

"None," Carol said. "I've not made any enemies lately."

"But you have been investigating the murders," I pointed out. "You might have come close to figuring out who did it and they got scared and tried to scare you off."

"There's more in the bathroom," Rex said.

We went to see and there on the mirror, written in lipstick, were the words *This is for Natasha. You should have never let her be disqualified.*

"Wow." I looked at Rex. "You need to bring the Alpines in for questioning again. They are the only ones who would care about Natasha not being queen."

"I've got that planned," he said. "Mrs. Tunisian, do you know of any reason why the Alpines might want to threaten you? Besides the fact that Natasha was disqualified?"

"None," she said. "Other than I've been asking questions about the murders." She frowned. "Do you think the Alpines want me to stop?"

"What have you been asking around about?" Rex asked.

"The sewing circle," Carol and I said at the same time.

"Patricia and Winona were both in the sewing circle and were pushing their weight around," I said.

"Come to think of it, Helen Alpine is also in the sewing circle," Carol said. "I need to ask Francine Fikel—she's a long-time member—if Helen was at odds with Winona or Patricia."

"Why does Helen worry you? Is she a good shot?" I asked. "Does she own a handgun?"

"Those are questions for me to ask," Rex said. "I think if there's one thing to learn from this, ladies, is that it's not safe for you to be investigating."

There was a short knock at the door and Officers Brown and Lasko walked in with Shane. "Wow," Megan said. "This is a mess."

"There's a couple of threats," Rex said as we walked back into the kitchen. "I think Mrs. Tunisian interrupted them because they only got to the back of the house. The front seems untouched."

"Lucky they didn't try to hurt you," Charles said.

"Allie, will you take Mrs. Tunisian to the McMurphy for a few hours? Mrs. Tunisian, are you all right with that?"

"Yes," Carol said. "It's probably best that I don't watch you go through my things."

"We'll be very respectful," Shane said and set down his kit. "It's going to look worse after I fingerprint the room," he said. "But I can give you the name of a good maid who can help with that."

"I'm sure I can do it myself," she said and put her arm through mine. "Come on, Allie, let's you and me and Mal get out of here."

"Yes, let's," I said. We walked carefully through the living room and went out the front door. "Are you okay?" I asked as we walked down the street. "That had to be a shock."

"I feel violated," Carol said. "My underwear drawer . . . I don't know if I can feel safe until we get this person."

"Who else is in the sewing circle?" I asked. "Maybe if we talk to them, they'll know something."

"I think it's the Alpines doing this," Carol said. "I heard that Natasha won a sharpshooter competition."

"Really?" I asked. "With a handgun?"

"Rifle, I think." Carol frowned. "But it's the same sort of thing, isn't it?"

"Well, Rex will bring them in and see if they own a gun and check it against the bullet from Winona and the casing we found from Patricia. I'm sure he will get to the bottom of this soon."

"Irma is in the sewing circle," Carol said. "They meet today. We can let her ask questions then and report back to us. In the meantime, I think I'd really like to lie down."

"Certainly," I said. "You can come to my apartment and use the spare bed."

"Thank you," she said weakly and squeezed my arm. "What would I do without you?"

"Mal will keep you company," I said. "Take all the time you need."

"First, I'm going to text Irma," she said. "The sewing circle meets at noon. I will be ready to get some answers by the time she gets back from there."

"I'll be ready to help," I said. "But for now, you nap. We'll figure this out." Hopefully before the killer makes good on their threat.

Chapter 24

I finished the first fudge demonstration and was upstairs in the office working on paying bills, when there was knock on my office door. I looked up to see Rex standing there. "Hello," I said as he walked in.

"Hi," he said, his face grim.

"What's up?" I asked. "Did you find anything at Carol's house? Are you questioning the Alpines further?"

"The Alpines have lawyered up and without evidence there's not much I can do there," he said. "I'm not happy you and Mrs. Tunisian are investigating. You've left yourself open to be a target."

"We just want to help. Now Carol feels personally attacked, she's going to work harder."

"Try to discourage her," he said.

"And if I can't?"

"Then keep an eye on her," he said and leaned against my door. "Also, I think it's a good idea if you take in Mrs. Tunisian," he said. "She's home alone this month and I'd feel better if she was staying at the McMurphy. You have really good security and are closer to the police station."

"I can ask her," I said. "But I can't promise she'll let me."

"Strongly encourage her," he said. "Do you have an extra room?"

"The McMurphy is full for the Nelson wedding on Friday and the Parrish anniversary on Saturday, but she can stay in my spare room."

"Thanks," he said. "I'll have police patrol the back alley once an hour until we find this killer."

"What about her husband?" I asked.

"She said he was gone for a month to spend time with a buddy on a Canadian fishing trip."

"Sounds like fun for him," I said. "But shouldn't someone tell him what's going on?"

"Maybe you can encourage her to make that call as well," Rex said.

It wasn't my place to make judgments on other people's relationships, but I wouldn't want Rex gone for a month while I was being threatened. I'd have to ask Carol if she could get ahold of him. Right after I asked her to stay. Rex was right. I needed to do what I could to keep Carol safe.

"Carol," I called as I entered my apartment and hung up my key by the door. She came out of the kitchen. The living area smelled of coffee cake.

"I hope you don't mind that I baked," she said. "I do it when I'm nervous or thinking about a problem."

"Smells divine," I said. "Listen, I just talked with Rex. He thinks you should come stay with me until your husband gets back."

"Really?"

"Would you mind?" I picked up Mella and petted her. "I've got the spare room and we've got really good security with cameras and such. Plus, if you're here, then the police only have to patrol the McMurphy and Michelle's place."

Carol sat down on one of the barstools. "I suppose it makes sense. I'm not sure I want to go back until my door is fixed and the place cleaned."

"I can help you with that," I said. "Mr. Devaney is great with replacement glass and I'm pretty good at cleaning."

"You're kind to offer," she said. "But I'm going to meet with Irma about the sewing circle and then start cleaning. I will take up your offer of Douglas's help if he's all right with it."

"Then I want you to stay with me. Have Irma come here after two and I'll help us figure out what, if any, clues can be taken from the sewing circle."

"If you're sure," she said. "I wouldn't want to be a burden."

"Are you kidding me? You make cake—who wouldn't want you as a guest?"

She bounced down off her stool and gave me a quick hug. "Thank you! That eases my mind. As soon as the cake comes out, I'll go home and pack."

"You shouldn't go alone," I said. "I've got a demonstration to do at two, but we can go together after we meet with Irma."

"Sounds delightful," she said. "Now go, scoot—get that demonstration done."

Chapter 25

I asked Douglas to fix Carol's door window and then did my last demonstration with Madison's help. I finished and was helping ring up fudge when I saw Irma walk in the door. Carol was downstairs talking to Frances.

"I've got to go," I said to Madison and took off my baker's hat. "Can you handle this alone?"

"Sure thing," she said. The crowds had thinned down to a trickle and I walked out of the fudge shop and met Mal in the lobby.

"There's Allie," Carol said. "Come on, dear, I have some coffee made upstairs and coffee cake as well."

"You're going to fatten me up," I complained a tiny bit.

"You could use a little meat on your bones," Irma said.

I noticed that Frances had a big piece of cake on her desk and a fresh cup of coffee. "Will you need me?"

"All's good," she said. "Go on."

I followed Irma and Carol up the stairs to my apartment at the top. "I hope you don't mind that I borrowed your spare key," Carol said. "I wanted to leave and didn't want to leave your place unlocked."

"Of course," I said. "Thank you for locking up." We walked in and Mella got up and stretched from her spot in the sun. Mal went running to greet her, but my kitty just jumped up higher on the kitty tree.

Carol was in the kitchen pouring us all coffees and slicing cake. I took off my baker's coat, went to the bathroom, washed up, and put on clean jeans and a T-shirt. I came out to find the two ladies at the table talking.

"You went to the sewing circle?" I asked.

"Yes." Irma sipped her coffee.

"Allie, sit," Carol said and patted a chair. "Have some cake and coffee."

I sat as instructed and took a sip of the coffee. The warm, smooth flavor went over my tongue and down my throat. "Lovely," I said. "Thank you."

"I was telling Carol that the entire sewing circle is nervous about this killer. Oh, and I heard you and Amy went over to Ashley's house and had coffee."

"We did," I said. "Ashley has some beautiful artwork in her home. We were talking about getting the artist to do some work on Main Street. Maybe a sculpture in front of the McMurphy."

"What a wonderful idea," Carol said.

"Was there any new information on a possible killer?" I asked. "Was Helen Alpine there?"

"No." Irma shook her head. "It seems Helen was with her lawyer at the police station. Rumor has it that she isn't talking about anything. Doesn't that make her seem guilty?"

"I would like to think she wasn't a cold-blooded killer," I said. "Maybe she's just scared of being blamed for something she didn't do."

"Who else would be angry that Natasha didn't win?" Irma asked.

"I don't know," I said and took a bite of the cinnamon blueberry coffee cake. It tasted so good. The warm berries burst in my mouth. "This is amazing, just like my Grammy's blueberry buckle."

"Thanks," Carol said. "I'll give you the recipe. What about Belinda, Natasha's mom? Is she part of the sewing circle?"

"No," Irma said with a sigh.

"We should go talk to her," Carol said.

"What if we let Rex talk to her," I said. "We need to stay safe."

"If we wait for Rex, she'll call a lawyer and not talk," Carol said. "I'm on the senior center volunteer committee. What if I tell Belinda that we want to nominate Helen for volunteer of the year? We can ask her some questions about Helen and Natasha and see how she reacts."

"I'm in," Irma said.

"Fine," I said, "But I'm going too."

"I'll make the call," Carol said.

"Let's hope we learn something," I took another bite of the coffee cake. "I feel as if we're spinning our wheels."

Chocolate Swirl Coffee Cake

Ingredients:
For crumb topping:
1 cup of flour
¼ cup of sugar
¼ cup of packed brown sugar
1 teaspoon of ground cinnamon
½ teaspoon of salt
½ cup of unsalted butter, melted

For the Chocolate Swirl Coffee Cake:
1⅔ cups of flour
1 teaspoon baking powder
¼ teaspoon baking soda
½ teaspoon of salt
¼ teaspoon ground nutmeg
1 cup of sour cream
½ cup and 2 tablespoons of butter, room temperature
1 cup of sugar
2 teaspoons of vanilla
2 large eggs
1 12-ounce bag of semisweet chocolate chips

Directions:
In a medium bowl, combine the crumb topping ingredients, stirring until just combined. Set aside.

Preheat oven to 350 degrees F. Line a 9-inch springform pan with parchment paper. In a medium bowl, whisk together dry ingredients: flour, baking powder, baking soda, salt, and nutmeg.

In another bowl, beat butter and sugar for four minutes until light and fluffy. Add vanilla and beat in eggs one at a time. Alternate adding sour cream and dry ingredients to the dough until combined. Pour half into the springform pan. Spread half the chocolate and topping on top and cover with other half of cake mix. Use rest of topping on top and sprinkle remaining crumb topping evenly over chocolate.

Bake 60 minutes until golden brown and cake tester comes out clean. Cool completely, remove from pan, and slice. Makes 12 slices. Enjoy!

Chapter 26

Helping Carol pack up was tough. When we arrived at her house, Douglas was finishing up repairing the glass in her door.

"You should think about getting a screen door," he said. "That way anyone trying to break in would have to go through two doors."

"That's a good idea," Carol said. "I'll call someone in the morning."

We walked inside and the kitchen was a mess, this time covered in fingerprint dust as well as making all the flour and sugar take on a slight gray tint.

"Why don't you pack for a few days' stay?" I suggested. "I'll start cleaning up."

"Okay," Carol said and visibly shivered. "I don't like the feel of my own home right now. I called Barry. He said it might be a week before he can get back. They are camping in the far north woods of Canada. He'll do his best to get here sooner."

"A week is fine, if you need it," I said. "I just want you to be safe."

Carol went to her room and I grabbed a broom from the closet and swept the floor. I used my phone to Google how to get rid of fingerprint dust, grabbed a pair of rubber gloves from under the sink, and filled the sink with hot, soapy water and began to scrub down the hard surfaces. The website on cleaning crime scenes said to do this on hard surfaces, but to vacuum up soft surfaces as soon as possible.

Carol came in with her suitcase when I was finishing the table.

"Is there fingerprint powder all over your room?" I asked.

"Yes," she said.

"Do you have time to run the vacuum? I read that you should get it up as soon as possible."

"Sure," she said. "I'll run the vacuum."

"On all soft surfaces," I called after her. "Even your bed."

"Got it!" she called back.

By the time we were finished, the sun had started to set, and my stomach grumbled for dinner. The kitchen was back to normal—well, as normal as a kitchen could be with missing dishes. Carol had righted her bedroom and put her sheets and blankets in the wash. It was dark by the time she was satisfied with her home.

"Come on," I said and put my arm around her. "Let's go to my place. This place is locked up tight and safe as can be. I don't know about you, but I'm hungry. How do you feel about pizza?"

"Sounds delightful," she replied.

"Only the best for my guests.

"Come on in," I said and opened the front door to my apartment. Mella sat in the window and Mal came running up with a happy bark hello.

"What a nice welcome," Carol said. "I don't know if I mentioned this before, but your apartment is so cute."

"Thanks, having to have it remodeled really helped me put my stamp on it." I picked up Mal, who licked my face. "If you remember, the spare bedroom is in here." I took her through the open living room/kitchen to the back, where the small hall held two bedrooms and the single bathroom. "You can bunk here," I said and flicked on the light. "I'll get you some fresh sheets and help you make up the bed."

"Wonderful, dear," Carol said as she set down her suitcase and took a look around. There was a queen-sized wrought iron bed in the center of the room, and a cheery white nightstand with a simple white lamp.

"There's a suitcase holder in the closet," I called as I dug out the sheets and a clean blanket from the linen closet in the hallway.

"Found it," she said.

I put Mal down and she followed me into the room. "The bathroom is down the hall. I'm up pretty early to make fudge, but don't feel as if you have to get up any earlier than you are used to. I'm sure you'll find it comfortable. I used to stay in this room when I visited my grandparents."

"It's very cozy, dear," she said and popped her suitcase on the holder, opened it, and started unpacking her clothes and placing them in the small four-drawer dresser painted to match the nightstand. I had placed crystal handles on the drawers to add a little shimmer to the room. The single window next to the bed was covered with sheers to diffuse the light.

I made up the bed while she unpacked. We worked quietly and I wondered if she was going to be all right with losing her home for the time being. I fluffed the last pillow and smiled encouragingly. "I hope you feel at home here."

"I'm sure everything will be fine," she said.

"Don't worry about the security system," I said. "I'll set it. And give you the code. All you have to do is not set it off in the middle of the night."

"How would I do that?" she asked.

"By going for a walk after I set it," I said.

"I'm not really prone to late-night walks." She closed her suitcase and stowed it in the closet. "Now, I know you mentioned pizza, but I would love to cook dinner for you."

"Are you sure? Pizza is only an order away and I don't have much in the way of ingredients in my kitchen."

"I remember," she said with a smile. "Ah, the single life. Let me make dinner. That will give me a chance to go to the store and pick up something yummy. I love cooking." She ran her hands together.

I shook my head and handed her a spare key. "Here's the key to the apartment. Please don't lose it."

"I'll protect it like my life depends upon it," Carol said.

"Good, because it just might," I warned.

"I'm off to the store," she said and grabbed her purse. "Are you sure you don't need anything?"

"I'm good," I said. "Tell Mary I said hi."

"I will." She opened the door.

"Be careful," I warned and stepped outside the apartment with her.

She rushed down the stairs. "I always am."

I closed and locked my apartment on my way to the office. It was certainly going to be interesting with Carol staying with me.

"Oh, my gosh, Allie, I'm glad you're here," Jenn said as I entered the office. "Things are crazy and I've got news." She got up and closed the door behind me.

"You're here late. What's going on?" I asked.

"Well, the Albright wedding is next weekend, and I've got a request for a second wedding and they are very close together. I'm not sure how we will handle it if they both want all the rooms. Plus, I've got news."

"Two weddings are good news, right? So why are you worried?"

"The Albrights want to stay longer and the Hendersons are coming in early," Jenn said, sounding out of breath. "I've got backup rooms at the Lilac Tree, but I'm afraid to give them too much of our business; they might outdo us."

"They don't have our rooftop deck," I reassured her. "It will be fine."

"It doesn't feel fine."

"It's not like you to worry like this," I said and drew my eyebrows together with a frown. "Are you okay?"

"Not really, no," she said and sat down. "Well, that's not true: I'm really wonderful, I think. I mean, I'm happy, but things are just off my schedule."

"What things?" I asked and sat down to do the bills. "Is there something I can do to help?"

"No, yes, no." She spun on her chair.

"You're making my head spin," I complained.

"My head is spinning, too." She stopped and leaned toward me. "And it's making me sick in the morning."

"Oh," I said. "Do you need me to cover for you?"

"Allie," she said. "I'm pregnant."

"What?" I felt amazed. "You just got married a month ago."

"I know, and it wasn't planned. I mean, we moved into our home the week before we got married, so it's been five weeks, really. We planned to have kids, but not for a year or so and then I started to feel sick in the mornings and so I took a test . . . you know, one of those early tests? And it said I was pregnant."

"Oh, Jenn, that's wonderful," I said and wrapped my arms around her. "I'm excited for you. What does Shane think?"

"I haven't told him yet," she said. "I told you first. I want to wait until he's not busy to tell him. In fact, I was thinking of having a surprise party. What do you think?"

"You want to surprise him with the news around a bunch of people?" I asked and sat back down. "I'm not sure how he would react."

"You don't think he'd be happy?" She collapsed onto her chair and frowned.

"I think he'll be ecstatic," I said quickly. "I just think that announcing it to him should be a private thing. You can still have the party. I think that would be great, but tell him first."

"Maybe you're right," she said and picked up her pencil and knocked it against her desktop in quick succession. "Huh, well, would you help me to plan the party?"

"Of course," I said. "I'd love to help. You can have it here on the rooftop or in my apartment. That is, when Carol Tunisian isn't staying with me."

"Why is Carol staying with you?"

"Someone broke into her home, tossed it, and left threatening messages."

"Oh, no!"

"I know, it was a real mess. It's where I was most of the evening, helping her clean up. Anyway, Rex thought it was best if she were to stay here with my top-notch security, since her husband is out of town."

"Oh, dear," Jenn said. "Do you think it was the killer?"

"Maybe," I said. "It's awful strange that Carol has gotten two threats and two people are dead. They are all connected by the festival committee. There just has to be a link."

"Why leave threatening notes for Carol and kill the others?"

"I don't know." I paced the office. "Maybe Carol isn't as much of a threat as Winona and Patricia. Maybe the notes are meant to stop us from investigating without killing again."

"This killer is diabolical," Jenn said. "Are you sure you want to expose yourself and the McMurphy to the threat?"

"Carol needs my help," I said. "I can't let her down. Now, what can I do to help you with the rooms for the overlapping weddings?"

Chapter 27

"So, how was your walk?" Carol asked me when I came in from my evening walk with Mal.

"Good, thanks," I said. "What smells so good?"

"You mentioned pizza, so I made my famous home-made pizza," she said. "Everything from scratch. We have mozzarella, tomato, and spinach and we have pepperoni and cheese. They'll be out of the oven in about five minutes."

"Yum!" I let Mal off her leash and helped her out of her halter, then hung them up. "I'll go wash up."

Carol set the tiny table that I had in the dining area. I usually ate at the kitchen bar, but it was nice of her to set the table. The smell of hot, fresh dough and melting cheese had my mouth watering. I washed up and came out to find her pouring two glasses of red wine.

"I hope merlot is fine," she said. "This is my favorite." She handed me a wineglass and sat down. The pizza was out of the oven and sliced to perfection. I took one of each.

"Wow, this is wonderful," I said and took a bite of hot, gooey goodness. "I should have had you stay over sooner."

"You're welcome, dear," she said. "I love to have someone to cook for and with my Barry away . . . well, it's been boring to cook just for me."

"How was your trip to Doud's? Did you see anyone?" I asked.

"Yes, I saw Mary Emry, of course, and sent her your regards. She had already heard about the break in at my home. Some people are speculating it's the Alpines, but others say it's someone else. Someone with a grudge against me."

"Who would have a grudge against you? No one from the sewing club, since you aren't a member."

"It means the sewing club might be a dead end," Carol said. "We need to look at the Alpines again."

"Yes," I agreed. "Let's keep you safe in the meantime and make sure my doors are always locked."

"What about the McMurphy?" she asked. "You can't keep her doors locked at all times."

"We lock after hours," I said. "In the meantime, there's always someone around downstairs. What if it's not the Alpines?" I leaned in toward her. "Who else could it be?"

"Not sure yet," Carol said. "It has to be someone with a grudge against the committee. The most likely suspects are the Alpines. Remember, Natasha is a crack shot with a gun. The girl's a natural at so many things."

"So, it could be Natasha after all," I muttered. "But it doesn't make sense that they would break into your home and leave threatening messages. I mean, why not just shoot you?"

"That would be awful," Carol said.

"What I mean is that it doesn't seem to be the killer's MO. No one else has received threats. What if whoever is threatening you isn't the killer?"

"Killer or not," Carol said. "That leaves me the next victim. I'm not taking that label lightly, either. I'm happy to stay here as long as you'll have me. I called Barry and he agreed that I could stay. He's able to head back home early and will be here in a few days, so you won't have me underfoot long."

"Well, hopefully Rex will figure out who is after you and catch them before that," I said. I noticed Mal was sitting patiently, begging just far enough away from the table that Carol could see her, but I wouldn't tell her to back up.

"I think we should investigate," Carol said.

"You always think we should investigate," I pointed out.

"We do a good job and can speed things up for Rex," she said. "Besides, my life is on the line this time. So, will you do it? I mean, you found the bullet casing when we went out and investigated the site."

"Yes, but Rex will not be happy if I do it," I said.

"But how could you live with yourself if something happened to me?" she asked.

"Nothing's going to happen to you."

"You don't know that," she said. "Look at the others. Nothing should have happened to them."

"Okay, fine," I said with a heavy sigh.

"Great!" She jumped up with glee. "Let's do the dishes and then put together a murder board. You've got the stuff for it, right?"

I shook my head and sighed. "Of course, I have the stuff."

Chapter 28

The next morning, I was up early so that the fudge would be finished, and I would have time to water the plants on Main Street. I was a day late, but they didn't seem worse for wear. I attached my hose to the spigot and used the spray wand to water until the plants dripped water. As I finished, I noticed Michelle walking by. It had been a while since our last meeting where she was to balance the books and I thought I would ask her if she needed any help. Also see if she was safe or felt threatened at all.

I wrapped up the hose and hurried after her. She walked up a side street to Market and then again up another street. Where was she going? I called out but she didn't hear me. I followed her all the way to the Alpines where I saw her knock on the door and enter.

What was she doing there? Oh, that's right—the Alpines were auditing the committee's books. I shrugged to myself and turned around. I'd pay her a visit later and see how she was holding up.

I stopped at the Lucky Bean and got coffees for me, Frances, Douglas, and Jenn. Then made my way home.

"Allie!" I turned to see Carol and Irma power walking my way.

"Ladies," I said. "I'm glad to see you out. But I'm not certain how Rex would feel about it."

"Oh, pish," Carol said. "I'm not going to live my life in fear. As long as I'm with someone I'll be fine."

"I guess that's all we can ask," I said.

"Besides, we're going to the senior center to see what the local gossip is and see if anyone might know about who broke into my house. I do have neighbors who usually keep an eye on things."

"Sounds like a plan to me," I said. "Keep me posted."

"We will," they said, and power walked away.

I left the hose outside in the alley and went in the back door of the McMurphy. "I have coffee," I said as I walked in.

Frances was helping someone check out. Douglas was working on the elevator and Jenn was nowhere in sight. I handed them their coffees and went upstairs to the office, where I found Jenn.

"I got you decaf," I said and put the cup down in front of her.

"Thanks," she said. "I'm so busy I don't know what is going to happen. The Albrights' wedding party has agreed to check out early, so we are good to go for a Saturday wedding on the beach."

"Sounds great," I said.

She leaned back in her chair. "How's having Carol at your house working out?"

"She makes a mean coffee cake and last night she made homemade pizza. I'm going to gain ten pounds."

"You will not," she said.

"Have you told Shane yet?" I asked.

"Not yet. I want to wait until I'm two months," she said. "What if I lose it and he gets his hopes dashed?"

"He should know, because if you lose the baby you will need him more than ever. But let's not talk about losing the baby. It's early days. Let's keep things light and happy."

"You're right," she said. "As usual. I'll tell him soon."

"Have you been to the doctor yet?"

"I have an appointment scheduled in two weeks," she said. "I'm still excited."

"You should be," I said. "What a wonderful thing."

"Speaking of wonderful things, how's it going with you and Rex?"

"We haven't seen much of each other. He's busy with the investigation and now I have Mrs. Tunisian staying with me."

"Any further word from Melonie?"

"She's been off-island taking care of her mother," I said. "Which means that it's been nice and quiet."

"Except for two murders and a break-in," Jenn pointed out. "How's the investigation going?"

"Not well," I said. "It all seems to point to the Alpines, but they aren't talking, and we have no evidence."

"The senior network isn't working this time?"

"No." I shook my head and sighed. "No one saw anything except Patricia, and she's gone."

"What did she see again?"

"A person with silver fairy wings talking to Winona on the pier where she was killed."

"Well, have you made a list of people wearing silver fairy wings?"

"No," I said and frowned. "How could I? There were too many to remember."

"Pictures, my dear," Jenn said. "I've got hundreds of pictures I took on my cell phone and I bet I'm not the only one. I'll upload mine to the web and send you the link. Maybe you can keep Mrs. Tunisian busy identifying people and making a list."

"Now that sounds promising," I said. "Thanks!"

"You're welcome," she said. "Maybe we can catch a killer yet."

"Fingers crossed," I replied. "Fingers crossed."

Chapter 29

After my afternoon fudge making demonstration, I got cleaned up and decided to go see Michelle. It had been a day since Carol's break-in, and I needed to know if Michelle was all right. Besides, she might have pictures of that night as well. I'd gotten a few from Mrs. Tunisian and she went back to the senior center to see if anyone else had pictures from that night.

I took Mal with me on the walk to Michelle's. She was out in her garden working when we stopped by. "Hi, Michelle," I said from over the top of her three-foot-tall picket fence. "How are you?"

She looked up from her garden and sat back on her heels. "Hi, Allie, I'm doing okay."

"I was checking in on you. You see, Carol Tunisian's home was broken into yesterday and she got more threats. I just want to make sure you are fine."

"I'm good," she said. "No break-ins here." She stood and walked over to us. "Do you have any idea who is doing it? Is it Winona's killer?"

"We have no idea," I said. "Weird, though, that it's only Carol being threatened when Amy and you and I are on the committee as well."

"Well, I've been home a lot," she said. "I have no idea why Amy might not be targeted unless she's the one doing it. I heard she accused someone of sleeping with her husband recently. She might be the jealous type. Have you looked into her?"

"No," I said and tilted my head. "I don't think she's involved. I'm glad you feel good about things here. I want you to stay safe. How was your visit with the Alpines today?"

"What do you mean?"

"I saw you in the street and tried to say hi, until I saw you go into the Alpines. I assume it was for auditing the books for the festival. Right? Did they treat you right? I mean, they seem to be a suspect in the threats."

"Threats? Plural?"

"Yes, the note I told you about and then the message left on the mirror during the break-in."

"What did the threat say?"

"Something about being angry that Natasha didn't make queen," I said. "I don't know exactly, as the police got there and messed up things with fingerprint powder before I got there."

"Did they find any fingerprints?" she asked and put her hand to her throat. "I hope so. Then they can identify the killer."

"Or at least the person who broke in and left the threats,"

I said. "But, of course, only if they have the fingerprints on record."

"Oh, so it won't work if the killer has never been fingerprinted before? Sad," she said. "What can I do to help?"

"Maybe stay away from the Alpines for a while until we sort this all out," I said. "Sound good?"

"Certainly," she said. "They'll take a week or two to audit the books, so I'll steer clear of them."

"Thanks," I said. "Stay safe and Rex will keep you updated if he figures out who is threatening us."

"Stay safe yourself," she said and gave Mal a pat on the head. "Bye."

"Come on, Mal," I said. "Let's go check on Amy."

Arf!

We walked a half mile or so and rounded a corner to see Amy coming out of her home. She had a smile on her face. "Hi, Amy," I said, waving at her.

"Allie!" She waved back. "What's going on?"

"Did you talk to Rick about the sculptures?"

"Yes," she said, "and I was embarrassed when he found out I thought he was having an affair. I'm so happy it was only art and not something worse."

"What does he think of you having a threat over your head?"

"He's keeping a close eye out in the evenings. I'm pretty sure no one would try to hurt us in the light of day."

"I wouldn't say that," I concluded. "Patricia was murdered in the daytime."

"Oh, dear, that's right," she said.

"I think it's best if you don't go anywhere alone."

"What about you?" she asked. "You're on the committee, too."

"Now," I said, "but I wasn't on it when Natasha was disqualified."

"Do you still think it's the Alpines going after us for that reason? Isn't it silly at this point?"

"I suppose you do have a point," I said. "But still, just to be safe, you shouldn't go out alone and I should get back to the McMurphy."

Just then I heard the boom of the cannon and Amy looked at me funny. "Allie . . ." She collapsed in my arms. I noted that she was shot in the shoulder. Another shot rang out, bouncing off the sidewalk near Mal. She barked and rushed to the safety of the fence.

I dragged Amy inside her fence and hunkered down. No more shots happened. I grabbed my phone and dialed 911.

"This is 911, what is—"

"Charlene, it's Allie. Amy Houseman has been shot."

"Oh, my goodness. Where are you? Is she all right?"

"She's bleeding badly," I said and tore a length of cloth off my T-shirt and pressed it into the wound. "Send the ambulance. Also, there was a second shot and I'm not sure if the shooter is still out there."

"Stay on the line with me," she said. "The police and ambulance are on their way."

"Let them know that the shooter could still be out there," I said. "I don't want anyone else shot."

"I'll let them know," she said. "Don't worry. How's Amy? Does she have a pulse?"

"She does," I said. "But it's weak and she's losing a lot of blood."

"You should hear the siren in the distance."

I did hear it faintly and getting louder. "Hopefully, that

will chase the shooter away," I said. Two officers on bikes came screeching up. They set the kickstand on their bikes and hurried toward us. It was Charles and Rex.

"Get down," I said. "The shooter might still be there."

They hunkered down and ran to us. "What happened?" Rex asked.

"We were standing on the sidewalk talking when the cannon boomed on the hour and then Amy looked at me and collapsed. But the shooter didn't even hide a second shot. It bounced off the sidewalk next to Mal."

"Brown, call for Lasko and you two go search the area."

"Yes, sir," Charles said, and crab-walked around the corner out of the line of sight. The ambulance showed up and George and Tim Jones came out with a stretcher and headed toward us.

"Keep low," Rex called. "There may still be an active shooter."

They ducked down and came around the fence and out of the line of sight. George took over and left me to watch with my hands covered in blood.

"We have to take her now. She's serious. Tim, call a life flight. We're going to have to get her off the island and into surgery."

"Yes, sir," Tim said.

George started a saline drip and packed the wound as best he could. The two men put her on a stretcher as her husband Rick came running up the sidewalk.

"I heard something was going on at my house. Oh, gosh, Amy!" he cried. "What happened?"

"She was shot," I said.

"We're going to life flight her to Cheboygan," George said. "Rex, cover us as we put her in the ambulance."

Rex stood with his gun at the ready, but there was no sign of a shooter. The two EMTs and Rick put Amy in the ambulance and roared off to the airport. The silence was deafening after they left. I found myself still sitting on the ground, worrying over a friend.

"All's clear," Charles said as he came around. "We found shell casings. It looks like they used a rifle this time."

"This is terrible," I said.

"What were you and Amy doing?" Rex asked.

"I was checking on her," I said. "This makes the third person on the committee hurt. We need to really watch over Michelle and Carol."

"And you," Rex said and helped me up. "Come on, let's get you home. Then I'm going to need a full witness report."

"There wasn't much to witness," I said. "We were standing there talking when the cannon went off and I saw that Amy was hurt. Then there was a second shot, but it hit the sidewalk, just missing Mal. If this were a sharpshooter, they wouldn't have missed."

"Unless they were warning you," he said. "You need to stop investigating."

"No," I disagreed. "I think I need to investigate even more now."

"I'm going to bring Natasha Alpine in," Rex said. "She's a sharpshooter and may know someone in the community who might have done this."

"Or she might have done this," I said. "Good luck getting her to talk."

"It's all I can do, Allie, until I can match evidence to a person. The motive is not that clear. Why go after people when the pageant is over?"

"Anger," I said. "People stew over disappointment. You should question her mother as well."

"I'll do that," he said. "Now let's get you home. I'd feel better if you didn't go for any more walks alone."

"I wasn't alone when this happened," I pointed out as we walked his bike to the McMurphy. "Plus, Mal needs her walks."

We got to the McMurphy and when we walked in the back Frances and Carol came running to me.

"Allie, we heard," Frances said. "Are you all right?"

"I'm fine," I said. "Just a little shook up." I took Mal off her leash and harness and let her run to her water bowl.

"How is Amy?" Carol asked.

"She was life flighted to Cheboygan," I said.

"I think it's best if you ladies don't take walks until we figure out who is doing this," Rex said.

"What about Mal?" I asked.

"I'll come walk her," Rex said. "Or Douglas can walk her."

I frowned. "I don't like being on house arrest."

"Honey, you could have been hurt," Frances said and put her arm around my shoulder. "Let's do what Rex says for a while, okay?"

"Fine," I said and tried not to pout. But how was I supposed to investigate if I couldn't leave the McMurphy?

Chapter 30

"I think we should work on the murder board," I said later that night. It was after dinner and Rex had just left after walking Mal. "I want to find this killer so I can get back to my life."

"I agree," Carol said. She pulled out the thick poster board she'd put up on an easel. "I had this ready in my room."

"Great," I said. "What do we know?"

"What we know is that Winona was killed the night of the festival bonfire and pushed into the water," Carol said and stuck a picture of Winona from the paper onto the bulletin board I had brought out.

"Where did you get the pictures?" I asked. "Have you been holding onto them for a murder board?"

"Maybe," she said. "Not the point. Next, I got a threatening note, then Patricia was killed by the school and dragged into the lilac bushes. After that, my home was broken into and then today Amy was shot." She posted a picture of Amy from the committee photo that had been in the paper for the article declaring the new festival back in February. "Only Amy wasn't killed, merely wounded."

"The killer is getting sloppy," I said.

"Or scared," Carol said. "It's hard to maintain a level of accuracy when you're scared."

"Have you shot a gun before?" I asked.

"Oh, yes," she said. "Went hunting with Barry a lot when we were young, but I got tired of tromping through the woods and gave it up."

"Huh," I said. "How many others do you think shot a gun before?"

"Pretty much everyone on the island," Carol said.

"That's a lot of suspects," I said. "Let's try to narrow it down."

"Well, all of the victims are on the festival committee and were judges for the parade and the pageant."

"We already know that the Alpines have motive for the pageant, but there's no proof they are involved," I said.

"We also know that Natalie is a sharpshooter; it was part of her talent last year in the Miss Mackinac Island pageant."

"Again, there's no gun," I said.

"Right, only a shell casing and that's from a semiautomatic weapon."

I shifted in my seat and Mal adjusted from her curled-up position in my lap. "Who would bring a semiautomatic weapon to a bonfire?"

"Could have been anyone." Carol tapped her fingers on her chin. "We could try to figure out who owns one on the island."

"I think that's something for official records and Rex will have that information."

"You should get it from him," she said.

"I can't," I sighed. "He would never talk to me about an open case. At least not any more than he'd tell the press."

"Well, I think this is a crime of passion," Carol announced.

"Why?" I asked. "It seems more like your fellow committee members were stalked, then shot in a moment of passion, except for maybe Winona."

"Maybe there are two killers," she said. "One crime of passion and one calmly calculating."

"That would not be good," I said. "How about we stick to one killer with different moods. Maybe they meant to miss Amy. Maybe they like Amy and spared her."

"Let's hope they like me too," Carol said. "Okay, we have victims, we have means, what we need is motive."

"You mean besides the Alpines," I said and pointed to the picture she had put up of a smiling Natasha and her mom and grandma at the Lilac Festival.

"We can't rule them out," Carol said. "But I assume that if they were guilty, Rex would have found out already."

"Then who? Who else would want the committee taken out? Did you stiff a vendor? Steal someone's ideas?"

"I don't think so," Carol said. "All the meetings were open to the public, so if an idea wasn't ours, it was given its due in public. As for the vendors, we took bids, so it was completely fair."

"Then there must have been something else you guys did to make the killer mad."

"I just don't know." Carol scrunched up her mouth. "I tried using the senior center gossip line. The center was abuzz about today's shooting, but it was all speculation. No one saw Patricia the morning she died. No one witnessed Amy's shooting. And if anyone is angry at the committee, they are keeping it to themselves."

"Well, that right there is telling," I said thoughtfully. "I mean, the killer is not on the local gossip circuit. Maybe it's an off-islander. You know, from St. Ignace or Mackinaw City."

"If that's the case, then figuring out who did it will be next to impossible."

"Right," I said. "We can test the theory. If they live off-island, they most likely arrived by ferry. So that doesn't fit because the bonfire was after the ferries quit running for the evening."

"But Patricia was murdered in the morning, so they could have stayed the night of the festival and then come back on the ferry the day they killed Patricia. Also, Amy was hurt after ten, so the killer could still be an off-islander."

"But what motive would an off-islander have to hurt you?" I asked.

"You're right," Carol said and paced the room. "I don't know anyone who would want to hurt me that also lives off the island. So, it was definitely a local. I'm going to have to dig into this further."

"Why don't we sleep on it?" I suggested.

"Sleuthing is certainly harder than I thought," she said. "I need a cup of tea before bed. Would you like one?"

"Yes, please," I said. Maybe, just maybe the thorny problem of motive would discourage Carol from further investigation.

Chapter 31

As I made fudge the next morning, I thought about who might have had a reason to hurt Amy and Carol. If Carol was truly the next victim, then the suspect would have to have a personal motive. Working on a festival was challenging and Carol and the others did it on a volunteer basis. Who would want to kill volunteers?

I finished filling my counter by the time Frances arrived at eight a.m.

"Good morning," she said. "How are you and Carol getting along?"

"Good," I said. "We worked on a murder board, but we're stuck on motive. Who is local who would want to kill festival volunteers?"

"That's a good question," Frances said. "Did you think about scorned vendors or someone who might have wanted to be on the committee or in charge who didn't get invited in?"

"We thought of vendors, but not someone who might have felt slighted over the committee membership. But the real question is why would a slight like that set someone off into murder?"

"Has Rex talked to Amy yet? Maybe she can shed some light."

"I don't know," I said. "I haven't heard from him. He's supposed to come walk Mal any time now. I'll ask him if he talked to Amy. But I doubt she saw anything. I didn't and I was facing the shooter. Rex said he was going to talk to the Alpines. Maybe they could shed light on this."

"Do you think he'd tell you if they had?" Douglas asked as he came in from the back door.

"Probably not," I said. "But he'd definitely let me know if he was close to solving the case. Which reminds me," I said. "I need to call Michelle. She's alone and the only member of the committee not here." I took off my hat and my chef's coat. "In fact, I think I'll walk Mal and go see Michelle myself."

"You are not going out there alone." Frances put her foot down.

"I'll go with her," Carol said as she came down the stairs.

"But that puts all three of you in the same place," Douglas pointed out.

"How would the killer know unless they were stalking us?" I said. "If they are stalking us, then that is a clue in itself."

"Right, because only a local or an overnight guest would

be on island at this time in the morning," Carol said. "It would narrow down the pool of suspects."

I put Mal in her harness and clipped on her leash. "If we're not back when Rex comes by, let him know we're on our way home. Okay?"

"Well," Frances frowned at us. "Just don't get hurt."

"We won't," Carol assured her, and we hurried out the door. The last thing I wanted was to run into Rex on his way to walk Mal. We took the opposite direction down the alley and hurried off to Michelle's house.

The morning was warm and clear. Birds were singing and the horses' reins jangling as they started their day carrying goods to various businesses. Carol and I walked with purpose toward Michelle's house. We arrived about eight-thirty and knocked on the front door. But there was no answer. We knocked again when Mal started sniffing and went around the house. We followed her to see the back door wide open.

"Oh no," I said. We rushed into the house to find the kitchen in a shambles. There was a note written in the flour on the table.

You're next!

I picked up Mal so she wouldn't leave doggie footprints in the mess and to keep her feet from getting cut by glass.

"Michelle!" Carol called.

"Michelle," I called, too, and we went through the up-ended dining room and into the torn-up living room to the den, where they had pulled all the books off the shelf. "Michelle!" When there was no answer, I put down Mal and turned to Carol. "Call Rex. I'm going upstairs."

Carol grabbed my arm. "What if whoever did this is still here?"

"Right," I said. "I'll call Rex and we'll go up together." I hit Rex's number on my phone.

"Manning," he answered.

"Rex, this is Allie. Carol and I went to check on Michelle and someone broke into her house."

"Are you safe?"

"As best we can tell," I said. "We're going upstairs in case Michelle is up there and needs help."

"Allie, wait! Are you inside the house?"

"Yes, and it's messed up like Carol's was," I said.

"You need to get out of there, now." His tone was stern.

"Get here fast," I said and hung up the phone. "Let's go." We crept up the stairs, Mal in the lead. The foyer was fine. The bedroom on the left was a mess. Whatever they were looking for, they hadn't found yet. "Michelle?" I called.

We heard a noise coming from the back bedroom and hurried out. There, near the door, was Michelle. She sat up against the bed and had a huge bump on her forehead.

"Michelle, are you okay?" I asked and got down on her level. Mal licked her hand and sat down beside her as if to guard her.

"What happened?" she asked.

"Someone broke into your house," I said. "How's your vision? Can you tell me how many fingers I'm holding up?"

"Four?" She looked confused.

I glanced at Carol, who shook her head and then I put my two fingers down. "Call 911."

Carol went out in the hall to make the call. I put my hand on Michelle's arm when she tried to get up. "Stay down," I said. "You might have a concussion. Did you see who did this?"

"No," she said. "I was doing something . . . then I woke up with a headache."

I glanced around. "Were you hit by something?"

There was a line in the bump, and I saw that the edge of the dresser matched the line. "Did you fall?"

"I think," she said, her voice weak. "I think someone pushed me. I must have hit my head." She touched her bump and winced.

"The ambulance is on its way," Carol said. "I'm going downstairs to get some ice for that bump." Carol disappeared down the stairs.

"Don't move," I said to Michelle, then I stood and looked around. The dresser was across from the door, and beside a partially made bed. Whoever broke in must have stumbled upon Michelle, pushed her, then gone out. Still, how did so much damage happen to the house without Michelle knowing about it? The answer was in the pair of earbuds that were knocked to the floor, playing loud music. I reached over to her phone and turned the music off.

"How's Michelle?" Rex said from the doorway. I stepped aside so he could see her sitting on the floor, leaning against the foot of the bed with her head in her hands.

"They must have pushed her against the dresser," I said.

"My head is killing me," Michelle said.

"Here's some ice." Carol came into the room and handed her ice wrapped in a towel. "Put it on your forehead. You're lucky it didn't cut you or there would be blood everywhere."

The room shrunk with all of us in it, so I squeezed my way out, brushing Rex as I went. He got down on Michelle's level and talked to her in a gentle tone. I grabbed Carol's arm and pulled her and Mal into the upstairs landing. "On a scale of one to ten, how mad was Rex when he got here?"

"You don't want to know," Carol said.

George Marron came up the steps with his paramedic kit in hand. "We have to stop meeting this way, Allie."

"You're right," I said. "Michelle is in the back bedroom." I pointed the way, then took Carol's arm. "Come on, let's get out of here so they can do their job." I picked up Mal and we hurried down the stairs and through the kitchen and out the back door. Michelle had a beautiful picnic table sitting under an umbrella, so we took seats there.

Charles and Megan arrived in full gear. "What's going on?" Megan asked us.

"Someone broke into Michelle's house," I said.

"She was inside, and they hit her on the head," Carol said.

"Actually, I think they pushed her, and she hit her head on the dresser. Rex is up there now with George."

Charles moved into the house and Megan stayed with us. She got out her pad of paper and a pen. "Walk me through what happened."

We told her everything from the time we arrived until the time we came back down.

"So, you went through the crime scene twice," she said, frowning at us. "You should have called us the minute you found the door open."

"We wanted to make sure that Michelle was all right,"

I said. "She could have been lying there in a pool of blood."

"But she wasn't," Megan said.

"No," I said. "She wasn't. We did call Rex right away and then 911 when we found her."

Rex showed up at the kitchen door. "Lasko, see that these two ladies get back to the McMurphy in one piece, please." His gaze was flat cop gaze all the way and I knew he was roaring mad at us.

"All right, ladies," Megan said. "Let's go."

We got up and I glanced over my shoulder to see George helping Michelle out of the house. At least she wasn't badly hurt. The real question was why did the killer not kill Michelle or Amy? Were they just distractions or did they have a change of heart?

Chapter 32

"I heard Rex was mad at you," Jenn said as she sat down at the barstool. I made her a cup of lemon herbal tea.

"He can be upset," I said. "I'm still glad we went to check on Michelle. She could have been badly hurt like Amy."

"But she wasn't," Jenn pointed out.

"No, she wasn't," I said and handed her her tea. "That makes me wonder . . ."

"Wonder what?" Jenn asked.

"If the killer is done killing and now just wants to distract us with fear." I sat down on the barstool beside her.

"Why kill in the first place?" Jenn asked.

"It's motive that we don't have," I said. "But I think they killed Winona in the heat of the moment."

"And Patricia?"

"I think she saw more than she told me," I said. "None of the rest of us saw anything."

"So, you think the killer is framing the Alpines."

"It makes the most sense," I said. "There's really no proof the Alpines are behind any of this."

"It all goes back to the person wearing silver fairy wings." Jenn pushed a pile of photos at me. "I've printed off all the photos I had and that others had of the bonfire. There are a lot of silver fairy wings."

I sifted through the pictures, putting the silver fairy winged ones in a pile and those without in another pile. "There must be at least ten people with silver fairy wings, including Patricia herself," I said.

"Since she's dead, let's rule out Patricia," Jenn said. "That leaves nine people."

"That we have pictures of," I pointed out. "Then we have Amy and Michelle also wearing silver fairy wings, but they were both attacked."

"So that leaves us with seven possible suspects," Jenn said. "That's better than most investigations."

"I suppose that's true," I said. "Let's put these seven up on the murder board." The seven left were Sandra Winn, Emilia Karolek, Antoine Blue, Mallory Ludwig, Shani Engel, and two men I didn't recognize. "Any idea who the men are?"

Carol came out of her bedroom and studied the pictures. "This is Blake Schmidt and that's Andrew Johnson. Why do you want to know?"

"Patricia said she saw someone wearing silver fairy wings talking to Winona on the pier," I said.

"Right," Carol said. "Blake and Andrew work at the

Island Hotel. They may have known Winona from helping with the float."

"Then we can't rule out a man as the killer," Jenn said and sipped her tea.

"We could go ask them where they were that night during the fireworks," Carol said.

"I'm afraid if we tried to go back out today, Rex would have a heart attack," I said.

"Well, then we can call him and tell him to go talk to Blake and Andrew." Carol sat down on the side chair. "Tomorrow we'll go talk to the women. I happen to know that Sandy and Mallory are in the sewing circle and friends of Natasha's."

"Right, they might know more," Jenn said. "Good, we're getting somewhere."

There was a knock at the door, and I opened it to Rex. "Allie," he said and stuck his head into the apartment. "Ladies."

"Hi, Rex," I said softly. I refused to feel guilty for checking on Michelle. If I had to, I would do it all over again.

"Were your ears ringing?" Carol asked. "We were just talking about you."

"Really?" He raised an eyebrow and stepped into the apartment, making a beeline to the murder board. "What's this?"

"Our murder board," Carol said with pride. I shot her a look, but she kept going. "We've done a good job, don't you think?"

"Why are these seven on here?" Rex asked.

"Patricia said she saw someone with silver fairy wings

talking to Winona that night," I said. "We think that's why Patricia was killed. Jenn had a great idea and got as many candid photos as she could from that night and after we ruled out Patricia, Amy, and Michelle, these are the seven people left in silver fairy wings."

"Andrew and Blake both work at the Island Hotel," Carol said. "You should go ask them where they were during the fireworks."

Rex's mouth made a thin line and there was a twitch in his jaw. "Allie, can I talk to you in your office?"

"Sure," I said and waved him toward the door. He strode out and I glanced back at Jenn, who mouthed *good luck* at me.

I sighed. Rex was at my office door and I unlocked it for him and let him in, then closed the door behind me. "What's up?"

"I came by to check on you," Rex said and drew me into his arms. "You were in two very dangerous situations. I needed to ensure it wasn't three."

"I haven't gone anywhere since we got back from Michelle's. I promised not to go anywhere tonight."

He kissed my forehead and held me tight. "Thank you. I know how hard it is for you to stay in one spot. I also came to take Mal for a walk."

"Right," I said and stepped back. "But that's not why you wanted to see me in the office, is it?"

"You need to not encourage Mrs. Tunisian with that murder board," he said. "It's dangerous out there."

"Have you heard anything about Amy?"

"She's out of surgery and making a good recovery," he said. "I'm going to fly over to Cheboygan tomorrow and question her. She might have seen something you missed."

"I see," I said.

"And?" he asked.

"And what?"

"And you are avoiding talking about that murder board."

"You have to admit it was a great idea," I hedged. "Looking at pictures for silver fairy wings."

"Well, you missed a few," he said. "I happen to know Elias also had silver fairy wings."

"Is he your main suspect?" I asked. "Do you know why he would want to hurt Amy and Michelle?"

"I can only speculate," he said. "Elias claims he was home before the fireworks and his wife concurs—and by the way, she, too, was wearing silver fairy wings. She told me she's the one who made Elias wear them so they would match. Elias wasn't happy about it and that's why they went home early."

"It does seem weird to have guys wearing fairy wings," I said. "But I suppose there are male fairies . . . if fairies are real."

Rex blew out a long breath. "Allie, I need you to stop with the investigation. I can't look after you and solve this crime at the same time."

"I was with Amy and Carol," I pointed out. "I was never out alone, and someone needed to check on Michelle since she was the only one left alone. I should have asked her to come stay with Carol and me," I said and paced. "She might not have been hurt. How is she, by the way?"

"She's got a concussion and is being held overnight for observation."

"You're not going to let her go home alone, are you?"

"I can only strongly suggest she stay with someone else," he said. "I can no more control her than I can control you. Why is it that strong women think they're invincible?"

"Because we are," I said with a grin.

"Until you're not," he replied. "Seriously, Allie."

"I'll be careful," I said. "I promise."

Chapter 33

Careful wasn't exactly the word of the day. I was out at eight a.m. watering the flowerpots. I was worried that I didn't do a good enough job the other day and thought an extra drink wouldn't hurt the flowers. The thing is I had to do it alone, since Frances was working the reception desk. I figured it had to be all right. What killer would be out at stalking me at eight a.m. anyway?

I put the hose into the spigot and turned the water on and sprinkled the hanging pots. The flowers were lovely diamond frost euphorbia, bright mandevilla vine, and supertunia petunias. In the standing pots were summer snapdragon and Bolivian begonia.

I was at the end of Main Street watering the last of the pots when I had a feeling on the back of my neck that I was being watched. I looked around but there were only a few shopkeepers opening their stores. No fudgies yet prowled the streets and the horse and carriages weren't even out yet. I shook off the feeling and glanced down at the pot to see a glint of metal. There shouldn't be any metal in the standing pots. Someone must have used it for a trash can. I turned off the water and went back to dig out the metal. It wasn't trash. It was a gun. I didn't know much about guns, but this looked like a semiautomatic. I took out my phone and called Rex.

"Manning." He sounded as if he'd just woken up.

"Rex," I said. "I found a gun. I think it might be the murder weapon."

"Allie, where are you?" His tone had gone from sexy sleepy to concerned.

"I'm at the end of Main near French Lane," I said and looked around for anything out of the ordinary. "I was watering the flowers and saw a glint of metal. Rex, it's a gun in the flowerpot."

"Allie, are you alone?"

"Yes," I said.

He muttered something low. "I'll be right there. If you can, put your back to the building, okay?"

"Okay," I said, a little shaky. He hung up and I stood in the early-morning sun. Amy had been shot by a rifle. Was the gun there for me to find so that the killer could shoot me next? The hairs on the back of my neck rose up.

It seemed like forever before Rex arrived, but in reality, it was only five minutes. He wore sweats and jogged to me. "Allie," he said when he saw me. "Are you all right?"

"Yes," I said. "The gun is in that flowerpot." I pointed

to the pot. "I dug some of the dirt from around it just to see what it was and as soon as I knew, I called you and didn't touch anything else."

"Okay," he said and took a picture of the pot and the dug-out gun. Then he pulled gloves and an evidence bag out of his pocket. "Did you see anyone bury this?"

"No," I said. "Whoever did, left part of the barrel showing. It caught my eye and I thought it was trash. That's why I dug it up."

He carefully lifted the gun up and checked it for bullets, popped out three, and put it in an evidence bag. Then he put the bullets in a second bag. "Come down to the station with me."

"Okay," I said and wrapped up my hose. I walked beside him in silence.

"I thought you weren't going to go out alone," he said quietly.

"I was watering the plants. It's my volunteer work and only on Main Street," I said. "I figured I was safe. I mean, I saw some shop owners coming in, but there was no one else around."

We arrived at the police station and Rex sat me down in a chair next to his desk. "Can I get you a coffee?"

"Yes, please," I said. He put the evidence bags on his desk and went to get us coffee. It was a quiet morning. Only one other police officer was at their desk. I waved at him. He nodded back.

"Here." Rex handed me a cup of coffee with nondairy creamer in it.

I tasted it. It was hot and thick and surprisingly good. "Now what?" I asked.

"When was the last time you watered the flowers?"

"Just a few days ago," I said. "I was supposed to water them only once a week, but they looked like they could use it, so I watered them this morning as well."

"And you didn't see the gun the last time you watered?"

"No, I would have called you if I had," I said.

"Then, whoever ditched the gun buried it in the last couple of days."

"Maybe that's why they shot Amy with a rifle," I said. "Because they had already hidden the gun. I mean, it can't be good for a gun to be buried, right?"

"It's not optimal, no," he said. "Still, it seems odd that they would bury it in such a well-traveled space. It's like they wanted you to find it."

"But I wouldn't have found it until Saturday if I'd kept to the watering schedule," I said.

"The question is, Why would they want it to be found? And clearly, they wanted you to find it. Do you have any idea why?"

"I don't know," I said. "You tell me. Maybe they hid it with the idea of returning to get it."

"That's a thought," he said. "Maybe they hid it knowing you would find it."

"Gee, imagine if I hadn't found it. It would have been awful if some kid had found it first. You know they look into flowerpots and things."

"I'm glad you called me," he said. "Come on, I'll walk you back to the McMurphy and please promise me that the next time you go out to water the plants, you'll take someone with you. Okay?"

I sighed. "Fine."

"Thanks."

I hated being curtailed, but I knew Rex meant well. But who put the gun in the flower container? Why did they do it? Did we have any security camera feed of that part of the street? I knew my questions were also going through Rex's mind, but unlike him, there was little I could do about them.

Chapter 34

"Ladies, how is the sewing circle doing these days?" Carol asked the women sitting around the tables sewing as we strolled into the senior center.

"I brought you guys some fudge," I said and lifted my platter.

"What are you two buttering us up for?" Sandra Winn asked.

"We have a few questions," Carol said and sat down between Sandra and Mallory.

"You can keep sewing," I said. "We just want to chat."

"About what?" Mallory Ludwig asked.

"You both were wearing silver fairy wings at the Midsummer Night's Festival," Carol stated.

"So?" Sandra asked.

"Did either one of you stop to talk to Winona that night?"

"Do you think we killed her?" Mallory sounded appalled.

"Gosh, no," I said. "We heard that Winona was talking with someone with silver fairy wings, and we think they might be the last person to see her alive. We just wondered if it was you. If you might have seen something."

"The last I saw Winona she was with Michelle after the pageant," Sandra said. "I think they were going over stuff about the festival. Michelle had her clipboard."

"I saw that, too," Mallory said. "I think Winona said something cutting to Michelle because she dropped her head and walked off."

"Mallory, did you see anything else?" I asked.

"No, I had my five-year-old with me and he was so past his bedtime he took all my attention," she said.

"I saw Winona on the pier," Roni Clark said. She looked up from her stitching. "Does that help? I wasn't wearing silver fairy wings . . ."

"Of course, it helps," I said. "We're looking for any information."

"Well, I can tell you she was arguing with someone," Roni said. "I couldn't see who since it was dark, but I did see that the person was shorter than Winona and rather slight. If I were to hazard a guess, I'd guess it was a woman."

"Did you tell Rex this?" I asked.

"I haven't told anyone," she said. "I didn't think it was important because it was right before the fireworks started. Besides, I didn't see who it was, only the silhouette."

"It's okay," I said. "That's very helpful. Anyone else?"

"Gracie Hammerstein told me she is sure it's the Alpines. They were hopping mad the night of the pageant," Roni said.

"Do you agree?" I asked.

"Based on what I saw it could have been any woman. It's why I haven't come forward. There really isn't anything to say."

"There were quite a few of us there with silver wings," Sandra said. "Are you talking to everyone?"

"If we can," I said. "There were a couple of guys wearing silver wings, but I think we can rule them out."

"But you do think the killer was wearing silver wings," Mallory pointed out.

"All we know is that Patricia saw a person wearing silver wings and now Roni said she saw a woman with Winona. If we can find that woman wearing silver wings, then maybe we will be able to find out if she saw the murder."

"I tell you what," Mallory said. "If I saw the murder, I would be keeping my mouth shut. Everyone who saw anything has been murdered." She gave Roni a look. "It's not safe."

"Thanks, guys," I said and stood. "We don't want to keep you from your sewing."

"Oh, it's fine," Mallory said. "We're down a few members today anyway. You two take care."

I took Carol by the arm and dragged her from the group. We went out into the bright sunlight. "Well, that was interesting," Carol said. "Do you think it was Sandra or Mallory?"

"No," I said. "Not that they would tell us if they were the killer, but they both seemed genuine in their response."

"What about Roni? Did you expect that?"

"No," I said. "I would have expected her to tell Rex if she saw anything."

"Maybe Mallory is right," Carol said. "Maybe people who saw something are too scared to speak up."

"Clearly no one can identify the person on the pier with Winona," I said. "We're going to have to keep digging. Maybe look over those pictures again and see if we can see anything from the pier."

Carol put her arm through mine. "I'm for that," she said. "Now tell me, what's going on with Jenn?"

"What do you mean?"

"She was sipping decaffeinated tea and munching on soda crackers . . ."

"Huh, I hadn't noticed," I hedged. Then I had to think fast to dodge that subject at least until Jenn was ready to let the world know.

Chapter 35

"Carol knows something is up," I said as I went into the office and closed the door. "You have to tell Shane."

"He's working overtime on this case," Jenn said. "I barely see him, and I really want to make it special."

"Carol's pretty smart," I said. "I tried to distract her, but I'm not sure it worked. You know how gossip works on the island. Can you try to make it special tonight?"

Jenn sighed. "Yes, I will. I promise."

"Good, now what can I do to help with this week's wedding?"

"Can I put you in charge of the rooftop decor? Flowers are arriving at eight a.m. Saturday and my tummy won't let me be too with it in the mornings."

"I'm on it," I said. "Anything else?"

"No, I'm good." She wiggled in her chair. "I'm excited anyway. It's hard to sit on news like this."

"Hopefully, there will be a break in the case soon." I hugged her. "Tell him tonight, okay?"

"I will, I will," she laughed. "Or he'll figure it out when I'm barfing in the morning."

"I'll bring you some ginger tea," I said. "What do we have next weekend?"

"Another anniversary party. This one is a fiftieth," she said. "Much less work than a wedding, but I do love the brides."

"Me too," I said and went to leave.

"Oh, there's something else," Jenn said and picked up a piece of paper. "I took a message for you. It was from Roni Clark. She wanted to know if you knew that Elias wore silver fairy wings."

"Huh, I think Rex mentioned that, too," I said. "But he has an alibi for that night."

"Maybe his alibi person is lying," Jenn said. "You know some people would do anything for love."

"Yeah," I said. "How do I prove it?"

"Maybe go talk to him again; if he knows you suspect the lie it might push him to slip up."

"Roni also said she thought the person talking to Winona on the pier was a woman, because they were shorter and slight."

"Well, Elias is short, but I wouldn't call him slight. He's a gardener, after all."

"Maybe I'll go talk to him in the morning," I said. "You just never know."

"Don't go alone," Jen said. "Just in case, okay?"

"Okay," I said. "I'll go make you some tea."

"Ginger, please," she said.

"Got it, but remember, I won't be able to keep Carol from guessing," I said.

"Try, for me, please."

Trying was all I could do with that astute woman living in my home.

"Barry's coming back tomorrow." Carol rinsed the dishes before putting them in the dishwasher. "That makes this our last girls' night."

"I'm glad he'll be back, but you will be missed." I put leftovers in a container and put them in the fridge.

"It's also our last night to work on our murder board. And we need to look at the pictures. I've got several on my phone that my friends took that night as well."

"I'll make some coffee and we can look," I said and put on a kettle. Making French press coffee after dinner was always fun. The problem with drinking after-dinner coffee is that I went to bed pretty early because I got up at four a.m. to make fudge. Coffee and sleep rarely mixed. But I made an exception since it was Carol's last night with me. "Will you be glad to sleep in your own bed again?"

"I will," Carol said. "Not that your guest bed isn't extremely comfortable, it's just not my bed."

"I understand." I made the coffee and she finished up with the dishes. "I'm going to miss having such good meals. Thanks."

"It was my pleasure. Now let's get to work on those photos."

I brought her coffee and she set up her tablet to look at

the digital photos while I took another look at the paper photos. After all, the first time I looked at them I was simply looking for people with silver fairy wings. Now I was looking for the pier and Winona.

It took us two hours before we switched, and I looked at the digital while she went over the photos with a magnifying glass.

"I feel like a real detective," she said and waggled her magnifying glass. I laughed and went back to the photos.

A half an hour later: "I think I might have something." I zoomed in on a picture. There were some dark pixels that were the pier behind the stage. "Does this look like a person?" I pointed to a dark shadow on the pier. The light glinted off a pair of silver fairy wings.

"It does," Carol said. "Let me see that."

"It looks like a guy," I said. "Maybe Elias. He's shorter, I think. It's hard to measure perspective."

"That's definitely Winona's unicorn hair," Carol said and pointed to a figure stepping up to the pier. "She must have been going up there to meet him." She glanced at me. "Why meet him on the pier?"

"He must have wanted to speak to her out of the crowd," I said and looked for similar pictures. "Oh, here's another one," I said and pulled up a picture of two girls taking a selfie. In the background the silver fairy wings were indeed shorter than Winona's unicorn hair, but stocky like a guy, not a girl.

"Look how their hands are positioned," Carol said. "The body language. They were not happy with each other."

"Elias claims he went home, and his wife agrees."

"Well, not before he had a fight with Winona on the pier," Carol said. "We need to get these to Rex."

"I'll take them in the morning," I said. "What time is Barry coming in?"

"He'll be on the ten a.m. ferry."

"I'll be doing my demonstration," I said. "Can you send me these pictures and I'll text them to Rex. He can look at them and come up with his own opinions."

"And that's it? No more investigation?"

"Oh, no," I said. "We've still got other people to interview, and I want to go see Elias, myself. I think we need a heart-to-heart."

"I'd go with you, but Barry . . ."

"I'll have someone go with me, don't worry," I said.

"Not Jenn," Carol said. "That girl is pregnant."

"How do you know?"

"She's glowing, plus all the ginger tea. It's a dead giveaway."

"It could just be the flu," I hedged.

"Oh, come on, I know you don't believe it's the flu."

"Look," I said. "Don't tell anyone. She hasn't told Shane yet."

"Why not?"

"He's been working overtime on the case and she hasn't found the right time."

"All right, I'll keep her secret, but not for very long." Carol winked at me and yawned. "I'm off to bed. I've got an early power walk with Irma in the morning."

"Good night," I said and stayed where I was. I texted Rex the pictures. Then let him know that Barry would be back in town in the morning. Maybe we could have some "us" time once Carol was gone.

Chapter 36

"How's Amy?" I asked Rex. He'd stopped by for a coffee after my ten a.m. demonstration.

"She'll be able to come home today," he said.

"Wow, they don't keep people in the hospital long, do they?"

"Statistically it's better for people to be home. There's a higher infection rate if they are in long-term hospital care. Besides, her shoulder is healing well."

"Good," I said. "Was she able to tell you more about the shooting than I was?"

"No," he said. "She doesn't remember seeing anyone. Just the cannon boom and then pain."

"Whoever did it clearly wasn't aiming for Amy's heart," I said. "Maybe our killer is having remorse."

"I'm wondering the same thing," he said. "It seems like

Winona was a crime of passion; unplanned and angry. Patricia also seemed to be spur-of-the-moment, as she was not well hidden and there was the shell casing you found. Patricia's death was sloppier than Winona's and after that we've only gotten break-ins, threats, and near-misses."

"So why? I wonder. What is going on? Did you talk to the Alpines?"

"I did, and they tell me that there were at least six members of the sharpshooter group that could have been as good as Natasha."

"But you told them those members didn't have motive, right?"

"Motive is the real key to this," Rex said. "The killer wants us to believe that it's about the pageant, but I'm not so sure."

"So, you don't think it's the Alpines even though all the evidence points that way." I sipped my coffee.

"I've got no proof other than the threats that seem to suggest it was them," he said.

"And the gun I found—was that the murder weapon?"

"Yes, ballistics were a match to Winona's bullet. We only have the casing for Patricia, but it matches the type of gun, so it's highly likely it was the murder weapon in both cases. But Amy was shot with a rifle, which leads me to believe again that there are two people out there. Maybe the real killer and then someone trying to cover it up."

"Which could still be the Alpines," I pointed out. "Natasha could be the killer and her mother or grandmother are trying to distract us."

"By implying they did it?" Rex shook his head. "No, something else is going on."

"Did you take a look at the pictures I texted you last night?" I asked.

"Yes, and you're right, it does look like Elias, but there are no time stamps on the pictures, so it could have happened before he left like he claims. His wife still backs him up. Besides, why would he want to implicate the Alpines?"

"To distract us from him," I said.

"Right," Rex drank some coffee and looked thoughtful. "Listen, I need you to stay safe. Just because Carol is leaving doesn't mean you should go out for walks alone. Not yet. Things are really getting complicated, and I don't want you hurt."

"But so far I'm the only one who hasn't been threatened," I pointed out. "I think it's safe for me to go out."

"But they left that gun for you to find, and you were with Amy when she was shot. There was a second shot."

"That didn't hit me," I stressed. "Whoever killed Winona wants me to find them. They want me asking questions. Let me help."

"Allie, I'm not sure you understand the gravity of the situation," he said.

"I understand," I said. "I've been through this before."

"Allie, if we're going to date, you have to know that I need to protect you."

"I'm a big girl and can protect myself," I stressed.

He stood and frowned. "You can't protect yourself from a rifle. This is serious. Next time this killer won't miss."

"Unless they want me to figure out it's them," I continued to argue. "Look, our dating is a new thing. Let's not get all 'me Tarzan, you Jane' on this. You knew going into this that I get involved when my friends are threatened."

"Don't you think I feel the same way about you that you feel about your friends?"

"Of course, I do, but I don't tell my friends they can't go anywhere. They're adults. I give them options and then let them do what they're going to do."

He ran a hand over his face. "Why do I have to be attracted to strong women?"

I smiled. "Because you wouldn't really want someone you had to rescue every five minutes. Now, I've got to go help Jenn with some planning. I promise to do my best not to get shot and you need to promise me the same."

"Fine," he said. "I'm taking Mal out for her walk. I strongly encourage you to stay in and stay safe."

I stood and planted a kiss on his gorgeous mouth. "See you for dinner?"

"Tomorrow," he said. "I've got a bunch of paperwork to do, and the coroner's report will be on my desk today."

"Okay," I agreed. "Tomorrow."

He grabbed his police cap as I put Mal in her harness and leash. Then he took her out the back door and down to the alley. I watched him from my back window.

"What's a girl to do, Mella?" I asked my kitty and petted her. "Why am I always attracted to strong men?" I thought of Trent and how he tried to change me. Now Rex was trying to make me someone he could rescue. I sighed. Maybe I was better off alone.

* * *

After my afternoon fudge making demonstration, I decided to pay a visit to Elias. Even if he wasn't home, maybe his wife could shed some light on why he was so angry with Winona. Was it just because of the roses?

I showered, put on a sundress and some tennis shoes, then put Mal in her harness and leash and went down to the lobby.

"I'm off to see Elias," I said to Frances.

"Are you looking for a gardener?" Frances asked.

"No, I want to ask him more questions about his relationship with Winona."

"Where's Carol?" Frances asked. She sat at her reception desk, dressed in a flowy peasant top and long skirt, her feet encased in tennis shoes. Her short brown hair was perfectly done.

"Barry came by and got her," I said. "He's going to stay home now that things have gotten a little crazy."

"Oh, that's a good thing," Frances said. "Are you glad to have Carol out of your hair?"

"I think I'm going to miss her cooking," I admitted. "But I'm glad she gets to go home. It's tough having to stay in someone's guest room when your own bed is just down the street."

"She loved it," Frances said. "Barry goes off for months on his trips and leaves her alone. It was good for her to have someone to talk with."

"We did have fun looking for clues in Winona's murder," I said.

"Do you think Barry being home will really stop the threats and break-ins?" Frances asked.

"I certainly hope so," I said, then frowned. "I should

probably go check on Michelle as well. She's home alone after her break-in. Maybe I should have her stay with me now that Carol is gone."

"It might not be a bad idea," Frances said.

"Thanks." I waved and Mal and I went out into the crowded Main Street.

As I walked down Main, I checked the flowerpots and found they were still moist from my last watering. I didn't want to be responsible for overdoing it, so I left them alone. Mal and I walked down Main, greeting the storekeepers we saw and waving to the other fudge shop workers. Mackinac Island is considered the fudge capital of the world, so my fudge shop was in direct competition with four other fudge shops. It made for some interesting sales as we each tried to outdo the other in new flavors and products. Some of the fudge shops expanded into ice cream, but there were also ice cream shops on Main, so there was competition for that as well.

It was the fudge demonstrations that drew people in and sold my fudge. If I could find the time, I would add a third demonstration, but with just me and Madison there wasn't enough time to do it all.

We walked up past Market Street and into the neighborhoods that surrounded the state parks. Elias's house was a large Victorian that had been in his family almost as long as the McMurphy was in mine.

The yard contained a display of flowers and bushes that rivaled any flower show. I guess when you made your living as a gardener, you had to have the best garden in town to show what you were capable of doing. He had a small stone fence that was covered with climbing flowers that bloomed in purple and pinks. I opened the gate and Mal and I walked up to the front wraparound porch and knocked.

A woman looked out, then opened the door. "Yes?"

"Mrs. Sumner?"

"Yes . . ."

"I'm Allie McMurphy. I was wondering if I might be able to speak with Elias?"

"What's this about?" she asked. "Wait, you're the girl who does all those investigations, aren't you?"

"I'm a bit of a mystery buff," I admitted. "Is Elias here?"

"He's got an alibi," she said. "We both came home before the fireworks."

"I know," I said. "I was wondering if I could speak to him again."

"About?"

I blew out a long breath and picked Mal up. "May I come in?"

"Oh, yes, of course," she said and let us into the foyer of their grand home. The inside colors were gray and white and very modern for such an old home. There was an occasional table in the foyer with a huge arrangement of fresh flowers on it. "Like I said, he has an alibi."

"I know," I said. "I was wondering if he saw anything that night. I have photos that show him speaking to Winona on the pier where she was killed. It was clearly before the fireworks, but he might have passed the killer on his way to you."

"I see," she said. "Well, he's in his workshop around the back. I'll take you to him. Please follow me." She took me through the center hallway and into the back kitchen. The kitchen was done all in black-and-white with gorgeous tiles on the floor and backsplash. They looked original to the home. We stepped out onto a small back porch. I put Mal down and then followed Mrs. Sumner to a two-door carriage house with what appeared to be an apartment on top. Since there were no cars on Mackinac Island and the Sumners clearly didn't own any horses, the carriage house had been turned into a gardening shed. Although at the size of it, it could hardly be called a shed. It was more like a barn.

The door to the carriage house was open and she pushed on it. "Elias?" She gasped as she stepped inside. I followed quickly to see that the entire interior of the shop was tossed. There was dirt and plants everywhere. The lights were smashed and the workbenches tipped over. "Oh, dear." She put her hand to her throat. "Elias?"

"Elias?" I pushed past her and Mal and I searched for him, but he was nowhere to be found. The side door was open. I hurried out the side to see if I could find anyone. But there was no one. Mal had her nose to the ground and I followed her to the back gate of their privacy fence. It too was open, but there was no one in the yard beyond. "Elias?" I called.

"Did you find him?" Mrs. Sumner asked me.

I turned to face her. "No, I'll call Rex." I dialed Rex and he answered on the first ring.

"Manning."

"Rex, it's Allie."

"Are you okay?"

"Yes," I said, "But Elias Sumner seems to be missing and his gardening workshop looks like a mad bull went through it."

"Allie!"

"I just came to talk to him," I said. "You need to send someone down here. Mrs. Sumner looks so worried and frankly I don't blame her."

"Brown and I will be right there," he said and hung up.

"Good," I muttered to myself. First Patricia was killed and now Elias was missing. I was beginning to think that someone was taking out anyone who was on my suspect list. That means they were watching me. A shiver went down my spine. Maybe Rex was right. Maybe I shouldn't go out alone.

Cherry Cordial Pie

Ingredients:

17 ounces of sweet cherries—drained or thawed if
    frozen

¼ cup cherry liqueur

4.6-ounce package vanilla cook & serve pudding & pie
    filling mix

3 cups milk

1½ cup semisweet chocolate chips

1 precooked 9-inch piecrust (I used a chocolate cookie
    crust)

½ cup of heavy cream

1 tablespoon of butter

Directions:

Soak cherries in liqueur for 3 hours or overnight.
Make the pudding & pie filling as directed on the package. Cover surface with plastic wrap to keep a skin
from forming. Let cool about 30 minutes. Melt ½ cup
of semisweet chocolate chips in microwave (About 60
seconds on high, stir every 30 seconds until smooth)
and paint onto the bottom of the piecrust. Let cool or
refrigerate. Drain cherries and place in the pie on top
of the chocolate. Pour pudding carefully on top. In a
microwave safe bowl place heavy cream, 1 cup semisweet chocolate chips, and 1 tablespoon of butter.
Microwave on high 30 seconds. Stir. Repeat until chocolate and butter are melted and incorporated into the
cream. Pour on top of pudding. Cool for 4 hours.
Makes 1 9-inch pie. Enjoy!

Chapter 37

"Do you think Elias left of his own free will?" Rex asked Mrs. Sumner. They sat on the ornate couch in her formal living room while I stood in the doorway.

"I just don't know. I don't think so. I've tried calling him, but it goes right to voicemail. Can't you ping his phone or something?"

"That's not how it works here," Rex said. "I've got everyone on duty looking for Elias. Right now, what we know is that he didn't get on a ferry. It seems you were the last one to see him."

"What about the state of his work area?" she asked.

"Shane is in there now dusting for fingerprints," Rex said.

I handed Mrs. Sumner a mug of tea I'd brought from the kitchen. "Here," I said. "Take a sip of this. It will help."

She did as I asked. Mal sat beside her with her head in Mrs. Sumner's lap, trying to offer comfort. "What if he's hurt? What if that dreadful killer has him?"

"I'm sure he's fine," I said with more confidence than I felt. "The killer doesn't have any reason to hurt him."

"Then why make a mess out of his gardening area? Why is he gone?"

"I've called some friends," I said. "And the hardware store, no one has seen him."

"It's a small island," Rex said. "He will turn up and all this worry might be for nothing."

"I don't think it's for nothing," Mrs. Sumner said. "There's been so many break-ins. I read the newspaper."

"Let's not jump to any conclusions," Rex said. "Now, is there someone we can call for you?"

"I called my friend Myrtle, she's on her way over." Mrs. Sumner sipped the tea.

"Good," Rex said and sent me a look. "Allie, can we speak on the porch?"

"Sure," I said and Mal got up and followed me out to the porch with her leash in her mouth. My pup liked carrying her own leash. It was a cute trick, but it didn't seem to distract Rex.

"What were you doing coming over here?" he asked, his voice low.

"I wanted to ask Elias about the pictures," I said. "He might remember something from that night."

"Why didn't you leave that to me?"

"Well," I hedged. "I figured you have enough on your plate. Besides, he's not here and it could have been hours longer to find out he was missing if I hadn't come over."

"You got lucky," he said.

"Any idea why he's missing? Do you think this is connected to the break-ins at Carol and Michelle's places?"

"It seems like the same MO," he said.

"Except Elias wasn't on the committee," I pointed out. "And there's no threatening note. Do you want to know what I think?"

"I don't know, do I?" he asked.

"I think Elias remembered something. I think he figured out who our killer is, and they went after him like they went after Patricia."

"You think my Elias has been murdered?" Mrs. Sumner asked from the opposite side of the screen door. Her voice went up an octave and her face looked pale.

"There's no need to jump to any conclusions," Rex said and opened the screen door. I watched as he took her back into the parlor. Mal and I walked off the porch and did a spin around the garden.

"What are you looking for?" Charles asked.

"I don't know," I replied. "I just think that if someone wanted to kill Elias, they would have done that and left his body nearby."

Mal rummaged around in the bushes near me.

"We haven't found a body," Charles said. "For all we know, the place was ransacked without Elias inside. He could be at the hardware store."

"I called them," I said. "They haven't seen him." I waved my cell phone to emphasize my point.

"He could be over at a friend's house," Charles said.

"I called the seniors," I pointed out. "They are calling all of his friends. If he's somewhere safe, he'll be coming back within minutes or at the very least returning his wife's calls."

"What does Rex say?" Charles put his hands on his gun belt.

"He says not to jump to conclusions," I said. "So Mal and I are going to finish our walk. Can you tell him that for me?"

"I'm sure he'll want you to go straight back to the McMurphy," Charles pointed out.

"Yes, well, I'm a grown woman and last I checked this is a free country. Come on, Mal, let's go," I turned my back on Charles and went out through the back gate. I scanned the alley for footprints or drag marks. As far as I could see there were no drag marks. If the killer took Elias, then he must have been awake and walking. That, at least, was good news. The cannon went off and my heart skipped a beat. I think I ducked as I glanced around. No sign of any gunshots.

Maybe it was better for me to go home for a while. After all, I reasoned, there didn't seem to be any clues right now anyway.

Later that evening, I sat with Jenn in my apartment, sipping tea and talking about the day.

"I can't believe that Elias is missing," Jenn said. "It doesn't sound like the killer."

"No, so far they have only threatened or shot," I said. "Why start kidnapping now?"

"Do you really think Elias figured out who the killer is?"

"If he did, then they have to be tied to the roses," I said.

"Roses?"

"Winona's roses were killed with some kind of weed

killer the day of the pageant," I explained. "She blamed
Elias, but I spoke to him and he swore he didn't do it."

"Wow, then wasn't Elias a suspect?"

"Yes," I said, sipping my tea. "For a short time, I did
suspect him. In fact, when we saw pictures of him on the
pier with Winona, I suspected him again."

"What if he is the killer and is simply hiding his
tracks?" Jenn pointed out. "He must have gotten wind
that you were close to proving it was him and then he
tossed his place and disappeared."

I thought on that for a long moment. "You could be
right," I said. "Messing up his workplace might have
been a decoy to get us off the idea that he is the actual
killer."

"Also, Elias and Amy are friends," Jenn said. "It could
explain why she was shot but not murdered."

"But what is his motive?" I asked. "He doesn't have
any interest in the Alpines or Natasha winning the
pageant."

"That could have just been a decoy as well, to get you
off his scent," Jenn pointed out. She sipped her tea. "Hey,
I think I might be good at this sleuthing stuff, too."

I smiled at her. "Of course, you're good at it. You're
smart and unlike me, you know a lot of people on the island."

There was a knock at my front door. I got up and
peered out the peephole. It was Carol. I opened the door,
and she came power walking in.

"What do we have?" she asked. "Is Elias still missing?
Do you think the killer has him? Do you think he's
dead?"

"I don't have a clue," I said as I watched her pace my
living space.

"We were just positing that he might be the killer and faked his own disappearance to get Allie off his scent," Jenn said.

"Yes!" Carol snapped her fingers. "That is brilliant and would explain why he wasn't killed."

"But what is his motive?" I asked them again. "Why would he want to poison Winona's roses, then shoot her later that night? Why break into Carol's and Michelle's homes?"

"Elias and Winona must have had a disagreement," Carol mused as she paced. "Aha!" She raised her arm, her sweatshirt bobbing. "What if he wanted to have his roses win the master gardening best in show? That way he could get more business."

"But killing someone is not a good way to get more business," I pointed out. "And his wife claims she and Elias left the party before the fireworks. We have to remember that."

"But the pictures . . ." Carol said.

"Don't show fireworks in the background and could have happened before they went off." I sat back down and Mal curled up in my lap.

Carol frowned and paced. "He still could have done it. He could have snuck out and back to the party, shot Winona, and then gone back home before anyone saw him. We were all wearing masks and costumes. No one would have thought twice if he'd walked right by them."

"True, but if he is the killer . . ." I said. "Where is he hiding? He hasn't gotten off the island unless he took a small boat, and we all know how choppy the straits can get. A small fishing boat might struggle. Surely someone would have seen him in the water."

"Well, as far as the seniors are concerned, no one's seen him since he worked on Clancy Jane's garden this morning. He finished up the job just after lunchtime and packed up and went home. At least that's what Eleanor Sumner said, and Clancy agrees."

"Wait" I said and got out my phone and brought up a map of the island. "Maybe he saw something on his way home that he wasn't supposed to see. He would have walked down Algonquin Street toward Main. Did he go by Winona's? Yes," I said as I looked at the map. "Maybe he saw something there and put two and two together."

"Then why go home and have lunch and then go out to his gardening workshop without saying anything about seeing anything?" Carol asked.

"You're right," I said, disappointed. "I have no clue."

"Well, it's still light out," Carol said. "We can walk Mal and trace his day and see if we notice anything out of the ordinary."

"That's a great idea," I said. "Jenn, do you want to come?"

"Not this time," Jenn said. "Shane will be home for dinner tonight and I want to talk to him."

"About your pregnancy?" Carol asked. "It's about time, dear."

"How did you know?" Jenn asked and looked from Carol to me. "Did you tell her?"

"No, she didn't tell me," Carol said. "I figured it out with the ginger tea and your glowing face. Congrats, by the way."

"I told her not to say anything to anyone," I said.

"And I haven't," Carol said. "At least not until you tell your hubby. Then I'll be on the phone lightning quick."

"I wish you guys would stop pushing me," Jenn grumbled. "I'm telling him soon. It's not like I'm keeping it from him."

"We will stop pushing," I said and gave Carol a look.

"Of course," Carol said. "Whatever you need. We're here for you."

"Why don't you two go on your walk," she said. "I'll be fine."

"I'm sure you will," I said. "Come on, Carol, let's get out of her hair."

"Be safe, you two," Jenn said.

"We always are," I replied, and then I knocked wood. I mean, what could go wrong?

Chapter 38

Mal and Carol and I walked up the street, keeping an eye on the houses and the bushes. Mal had her nose down and was sniffing her way along Algonquin Street.

"Hey, look," I said. "There's Michelle's house. We should go check on her."

"I agree," Carol said. "I wonder how her head is and if she's being safe with a killer still around."

We walked up to find Michelle out in her yard using a tool to pop weeds out of her lawn. It was a perfect lawn, so the weeds were few and far between. "Hi, Michelle," I said.

"Allie, Mrs. Tunisian, how are you?" she asked and picked up the tool and walked toward us.

"We're good," I said. "How's your head?"

"Well, you know, still sore and the bump might take a day to go away, but I'm fine."

"Are you sleeping at night?" Carol asked. "Because I couldn't after my break-in and I was staying at Allie's, so I wasn't alone."

"It's been a bit of a struggle," Michelle said and rubbed her head. "It took me two days to clean up the mess. I'd like to get my hands on the person who did it."

"You don't feel threatened?" Carol asked.

"No," Michelle said. "I feel angry more than anything. So, I'm taking it out on my weeds."

"Don't you use weed killer or something like that to kill them?" Carol asked.

"No, it's not good to put chemicals on your plants," Michelle said. "I find it better to use my tool. All you do is place it over the weed, stomp, and pull it out. I like the stomp part."

"Helps get the mad out," I assumed.

"Yes, it does. What brings you two down this way?"

"I'm walking Mal," I hedged.

"I'm with her so she's not alone," Carol said. "Did you hear that Elias Sumner is missing?"

"Really? Do you think it's related to our threats?"

"We're not sure," I said. "But someone broke into his garden workshop and trashed it like they did to yours and Carol's homes."

"Well, I can't wait until that person is caught," Michelle said. "They should have to pay for all the damage they have done."

"I'm sure they will," I said. "Say, did you happen to see Elias walk this way yesterday around noon?"

"I was working in my backyard around that time," she said. "So, no, I didn't. Are you investigating his disappearance?"

"No," I said.

"Yes," Carol said.

"Not really," I said and elbowed Carol. "We're just walking."

"Okay," Michelle said. "Enjoy your walk and be careful, you just never know who's going to come at you or from where."

"You are right in that," I said.

We continued our walk, but didn't see anything else out of the ordinary. "Maybe Elias didn't see anything either," I said to Carol. "He went home for lunch, after all."

"That means it had to happen in his workshop," Carol said.

"Or at least in his yard," I said.

We turned down Lake Shore Drive and followed it to Main Street, where the streets were filled with people and buggy riders and bicycles. "Thanks for coming with me," I said to Carol. "Do you need me to walk you home?"

"Oh, no, Barry's meeting me for a late lunch at the Boar's Head," Carol said. "You go on."

Mal and I left Carol and walked up to the McMurphy. I glanced in the window to see Rex talking to Frances and I realized I didn't want to speak to him just yet. "Come on, Mal," I said. "Let's go walk down by the water."

We continued our walk by the water and then rounded the road and I decided to go by Elias's home one more time. Why had the person who ransacked his workshop leave his backyard gate open? I know I didn't see anything when I looked, but it didn't make any sense. We walked down the alley and up to Elias's back gate. I studied it. It was closed, but I found if I got up on my tiptoes I could reach around and unlock it. I pushed it open and studied the back of the carriage house. Did the person who ransacked the workshop come in through the back or leave through the back? Maybe both, if Mrs. Sumner didn't see them at all. But there was no sign of anything untoward in the alley.

Mal started sniffing the gravel. "What is it?" She pulled me down the alley and around the corner of a neighbor's carriage house. There was a pile of brush and she dug through it, poked something, and sat with a happy look on her face.

I wasn't as happy. I squatted and pushed the brush aside. There was a hand, and it was connected to an arm and a body lying face down. It didn't take a great imagination to see it was Elias. I felt for a pulse. He was cold. So, I dialed Rex.

"Manning," he answered.

"Rex, I found Elias," I said. "I didn't call 911 because he's dead."

"Where are you?" he asked and I could hear him getting up from his desk and walking through the bullpen.

"I'm about a block from the Sumners' house. I'm in the alley near a neighbor's carriage house," I said. "Send Shane and George."

"On it," he said. "I'll call you right back."

I felt guilty not calling Charlene, but I was a bit tired of her asking me who I found dead and were they really dead. I moved the brush away from Elias and noted that there was a large hole in his back. He'd been shot. I was no expert, but I was guessing it was a rifle shot.

My phone rang and I startled. "Hello?"

"Allie, are you alone?" Rex asked.

"I'm with Mal," I hedged.

"Stay on the phone with me. Look around and tell me what you see. Do you see anyone?"

"No," I said. "But if he was shot by a rifle, then I probably won't see anyone." I moved so that my back was against the carriage house. I hunkered down near the brush and Mal licked my face. "I'm squatting," I said to Rex. "So that I'm not as big a target if the killer is out there. But I kind of doubt it. Elias is cold, like he was killed yesterday."

"It doesn't mean the killer won't be watching to see who finds him," Rex said. "I'm almost there and Brown is with me. I've got the ambulance and Shane on the way. Shane will take a little longer because he has to come in from St. Ignace."

"Okay," I said and hugged Mal.

"I'm at the alley. What color is the carriage house?"

"I'll stand." I stood and waved him down. He and Charles rode up and stopped in front of me. "Mal found him in this brush." I waved toward the body and the brush beside him and still on top of him. "I moved some of it to check and see if he was alive."

"Okay," Rex said. "Stay here with your back toward the carriage house." He took pictures of the scene and then he and Charles removed the remaining brush. Elias's head was tilted to the side and his hands were akilter. He wore jeans and a plaid shirt that was stained red around the big hole in his back. I swallowed hard. "He wasn't killed here, was he?" I asked as I looked at the white wall of the carriage house. "There's no splatter."

"He was definitely brought here," Charles said and took pictures. The ambulance showed up, its sirens wailing. The neighbors had started to come out of their homes to see what was going on.

"What are you guys doing on my property?" an elderly gentleman wearing jeans and a blue T-shirt said. His hair was white and his eyes blue.

"This is a crime scene," Rex told him and motioned for Charles to put up the tape. "Did you see or hear anything unusual yesterday?"

"What crime?" The man sounded worried.

"Elias Sumner's been murdered," Rex said. "Did you hear any shots or see anyone lurking around your carriage house yesterday?"

"I couldn't have," he said. "My wife and I were in Mackinaw City shopping yesterday."

"We'll need to speak to your wife, Mr. . . ."

"Grant, Joe Grant," he said. "My wife is Luna. She'll verify and we have ferry tickets to prove it."

"Good," Rex said. "Who knew you were gone for the day?"

"Anyone who was at the docks yesterday," he said. "We've lived on the island for years and know most everyone, except you cops."

"It's a good thing not to know the cops," Rex said and sent me a side-eye look.

"Who would have done such a thing?" he asked. "Someone who knew about my brush pile, I suppose."

"Not necessarily," Rex said. "This could merely be a convenient place to hide the body. We had cops all over Mr. Sumner's place yesterday when his wife reported a break-in and that he was missing."

"Isn't that the third break-in lately? Aren't you police supposed to prevent that sort of thing?"

"We're doing our best to put this perpetrator or perpetrators behind bars," Rex said smoothly.

George hunkered down next to the body. He rolled it sideways. "Looks like a bullet went in through the front and out the back. He was definitely moved, based on the variations in lividity."

"Where do you think he was shot?" I asked. "There isn't any blood here, but there also doesn't appear to be any drag marks. I would have expected drag marks like with Patricia."

"It could be the gravel is too hard to leave drag marks," George said. "Or they carried him here and covered him with brush."

"But he's a pretty substantial man," I said. "And we think the killer is a woman, so how would she get him here without dragging?"

"Maybe your killer isn't a woman," he said.

I blew out a deep breath. "The only guy on my suspect list was Elias and he clearly didn't kill himself."

"Clearly," George said with a stoic face.

I watched as George took photographs and then he and Charles put the body on a stretcher and rolled it into the ambulance.

Then I touched Rex on his shoulder. "I need to take Mal home."

"Okay, I'll come find you," he said.

"Do that," I said and gave him a kiss on the cheek, then headed down the alley looking carefully for any tracks or means to get a heavy male body to the site and dump him. Too bad people don't have cameras surrounding their property like the McMurphy. We might have been able to get something on camera.

At the end of the alley, I ran into Carol power walking toward me. "So, it's true," she said. "You found Elias."

"Yes," I said. "Mal found him."

"We didn't walk that alley," she said. "And I thought you were going home, not looking for bodies without me."

"I was avoiding Rex," I said, "and decided to try the alley again, looking for clues."

"I'm going to go see," she said.

"I wouldn't if I were you," I said. "The killer has a rifle and might be watching the site."

"True," Carol said. "Well, I guess we should both go home and stay there until this is solved. Oh, and you might want to tell Michelle to do the same."

"I will. Things are getting a little too hot for us. I think it's time to let Rex do the investigating," I said.

This time Carol agreed.

Chapter 39

"How's Amy?" I asked Rex later that evening. He'd stopped by and I cut him a piece of cake and made coffee.

"She's decided to stay with her aunt in Mackinaw City until this thing gets solved," Rex said, sipping his coffee.

"That's probably for the best," I said.

"It'd be even better if you stayed at the McMurphy and quit investigating," he said.

"You're starting to repeat yourself," I pointed out, slightly miffed that he might be right.

"You could have gotten hurt today."

I shifted in my seat and poked at my piece of cake. "I was out with Carol until she went home, and I thought I'd just look down the alley one more time. You were all over that alley yesterday. It should have been safe."

"Should it?" he asked and sat back.

"Do you think the killer put the body there after you searched the area?"

"They had to know that no one was home at the Grants," he said. "That makes them local for sure."

"Why kill Elias?" I asked.

"He might have figured out who the killer was and confronted them," Rex said.

"So why shoot him with a rifle? If he confronted them, then they had to shoot him face-to-face."

"Not necessarily," he said. "He could have turned around to come see me."

"Then he would have been shot in the back and he wasn't," I pointed out.

"Well, you found the handgun. Maybe a rifle is all they had left."

"Did you find out who owned the handgun?" I asked.

"It belongs to the Alpines," he said. "I've got them coming in tomorrow for questioning, but their lawyer keeps them from saying anything. I'm hoping being confronted with the gun will put some guilt into them and get them to say something, even if it's to deny. Once I get them talking, they just might spill the entire story."

"Do they own a rifle?"

"A lot of people own rifles, Allie," he said and finished his cake. "Until we find the rifle and match it, then we've got no case. Remember, we need actual proof."

"Right," I said.

"Listen, I have to go." He stood. "Are you okay alone or do I need to come back for the night?"

"I'm okay," I said. "I've got good security."

"You do," he agreed.

I stood. "Why don't you take the rest of the cake with you to the station. I'm sure someone would eat it."

"Thanks," he said and gave me a quick kiss.

I smiled, but my thoughts were on the killer.

The next morning, I finished my first fudge demonstration and left the shop to Madison.

"I'm not sure a glass storefront is the best place for you right now," Frances said. "That killer is shooting anyone who gets close to figuring out who they are."

"It's not like they are going to be on top of the roof across the street and sniper me," I said with more confidence than I felt. "Besides, we have cameras, and they would risk being caught on it if they tried anything."

"I'm glad this place has security like it's Fort Knox," Frances said.

"Where?" I asked.

Frances sighed. "Fort Knox—it's where they house the nation's gold. It was a saying."

"Oh," I said.

Jenn came sailing in nearly three hours late. "Good morning, ladies."

"Good morning," I said. "You're running late."

"I wasn't feeling good this morning, but I'm better now. Nothing some ginger tea and crackers can't fix."

"Ginger tea?" Frances lifted an eyebrow. "Are you—"

"Yes," Jenn said. "I'm pregnant and now I can tell you because I told Shane last night."

"Wonderful," I said. "Congrats!" I gave her a hug.

"Congratulations," Frances said and hugged her, too.

"How did Shane take it? Is he excited?" I looked at her

with concern. Not that I thought Shane wouldn't be excited, it's that I knew she was a bit worried.

"He was very excited and happy." She touched my arm and gave it a squeeze. "But we don't want to go too public until I hit the second trimester. Then we'll have a party to reveal the sex of the baby."

"I'm giving you a huge baby shower," I said. "But we'll wait until you're in your last trimester, so you'll be gorgeous in the photos."

"That would be lovely," she said. "We're going to need everything. My parents are going to flip!"

"Are you telling them soon?" Frances asked.

"Yes, I'm calling my mom tonight. Don't be surprised if she shows up here this weekend."

"That's not a problem. I have the flowers covered and the rest of the wedding will work like clockwork."

"I'm not worried," she said. "I'll do my job and foist her off on you!"

I thrilled at her happiness. It made me wonder if I ever wanted kids. Is that where Rex and I were going? No, it was too new, really, to think like that. I still had to work out whether I wanted to be his third wife. I shook myself mentally. Right now, we were dating, and it was fun and that was enough for me.

Chapter 40

After the second demonstration of the day, I showered and put on a sundress and decided to take Mal for a walk.

"Should you be going out?" Frances stopped me near the front door.

"We'll stay on Main Street," I said. "I'm sure the killer won't be shooting into crowds."

"You don't know," Frances said. "They've gone a bit over the edge with killing Elias."

"I think he confronted them," I said. "I'll be careful not to do that."

"So, you *are* going to look for them on your walk." Frances jumped on my words.

"No," I said. "I'm going to stay on Main Street in the safety of the crowds."

"Fine," she said. "Please be careful."

"I will." It was nice to get out and feel the warmth of the sun on my face. Mal, too, seemed to skip happily as we moved down Main Street toward the marina. I planned to turn around at St. Anne's and go to the other end of Main and do a big loop. I checked the dampness of the flower baskets as I passed and thought I should water them soon. I'd gotten off track, but they seemed to thrive regardless.

The crowds thinned toward St. Anne's church, so I hurried back toward the shops on Main Street. When we got to the lawn in front of the fort the cannon boomed, and I startled. Mal stopped to check on me. "I'm okay," I said. I looked up and caught a glimpse of Michelle hurrying up Fort Street. I was too far away to call on her, but like me she was out on her own. I wondered if she knew that Elias was found dead.

Mal and I cut through the lawn to follow Michelle when we ran smack-dab into Suzanne McGee. "Allie, how wonderful to see you."

"Hello, Suzanne," I greeted her as she hugged me.

"I wanted to tell you that I think you've been doing a fantastic job keeping the flowerpots watered."

"Thanks," I said. "When's the next decoration committee meeting?"

"The first Wednesday of the month," she said. "Be sure to come. We're going to be looking at August decorations and starting to talk about September and October."

"Of course," I said. "I loved last year's harvest decorations."

"Good, because I'm going to be asking you if you have any fresh ideas, so bring your thinking cap."

"I will," I agreed and hurried off toward Fort Street,

but there was no sign of Michelle. Maybe she went home. "Come on, Mal," I said. "Let's go check on Michelle. The way people are dropping, someone needs to check in with her daily." I tried not to think about what would happen if Rex found out I walked off alone. I mean, he could be mad, I suppose, but then I was getting used to that.

We hurried up Fort Street and took a side road into Michelle's neighborhood. I glanced around, making sure I wasn't being followed. So far, so good. We arrived at her front fence and once again I stopped to admire her gardens. "Michelle?" I called in case she was outside. When there was no answer, I opened her gate and let Mal and myself in. Her porch was wraparound and wrapped around a turret as well. I loved these old Victorian homes. They were beautiful homes. I rang the doorbell and knocked. There was no answer. So, I peered in the window and rang the doorbell again, then knocked. Still no answer. Maybe Michelle hadn't come home. "Come on, Mal," I said. "Let's go around to the back. Maybe she's working in her carriage house."

I stepped off the porch and went up the two-track cement drive to the back of the house, where there was a small back porch.

"Michelle," I called. I tried the back door. "Michelle?" No answer. At least the back door was locked and there didn't appear to be a break-in. That was a good thing as far as things went lately. I decided to try her carriage house and small shed in the back. The backyard was a small patch of green compared to the front yard and its flourishing gardens. I guess the front was for show and the back left plain.

I tried the carriage house door. But it, too, was locked. Next, I tried the shed. "Michelle?" I opened the shed and looked around at the bags of potting soil, the rakes, the lawn mower, and all the makings of a gardener's potting hut.

"Hello?"

I turned to see Michelle coming around the corner of her house. I closed the shed. "Michelle, I was looking for you." I tried not to blush. "I tried the front and the back door and thought maybe you were outside working."

"I was in the bathroom," she replied. "Why did you check the shed?"

"I was worried when you didn't answer."

"Yes, I can understand that, considering the last time you were at my home," she said. "Do you want to come in and have some coffee? I have cookies, too."

"Thanks," I said. "We'd love that."

Mal and I followed her out of the yard and into the house through the back door. Her black-and-white kitchen was a lot cleaner than the last time I'd seen it and it looked cozy. "Have a seat at the table," she said and started coffee.

I picked up Mal and took a seat at the small pine kitchen table. "I saw you walking down Fort Street," I said. "And it reminded me that we didn't talk yesterday. There was a big event."

"You found Elias dead," she said. "I read the paper. What a terrible tragedy."

"It was," I agreed. She filled two mugs with coffee and set down a plate of chocolate chip cookies.

She sat down and pushed a mug toward me. "Cream or sugar?" She pushed a cute cow cream and sugar set toward me.

"Thanks," I said and poured in cream, then pushed it back toward her and watched her add sugar and cream to hers. "I wanted to make sure you were doing okay. This killer is a nasty bit of business."

"I'm doing fine," she said. "My head still aches, but I think I'm getting over it."

"Rex said that Amy's not coming back to the island and Carol's husband is looking out for her. So that leaves you and me as single targets. I wanted to know if you want to come stay at the McMurphy until Rex can find the killer."

"Oh, I thought you were looking for the killer." She stirred her coffee.

"Not really," I said. "It's getting too dangerous. In fact, I'm not even supposed to be here right now, but I saw you on Fort Street and wondered if you wanted protection."

"You know, that might not be a bad idea," she said. "Give me some time to pack and close up the house and such. Can I say I'll be at your place after dinner?"

"That works," I said. "I'm glad. I'll feel better if I know you are safe."

"You're so kind," she said. "Now, let's talk about the festival committee and where we're at for next year's festival."

Chapter 41

"I've asked Michelle to come stay with me," I told Rex at dinner. "She's alone and on the killer's hit list. Now that Carol is with her husband, I'd feel better knowing Michelle was safe as well."

"It's probably a good idea," he said.

"How was your talk with the Alpines about the gun?"

"I shouldn't talk about an open case," he said.

"Who am I going to tell? I know you didn't arrest anyone, so what is up?"

"They told me they didn't know the gun was missing and that anyone of their household staff could have had access."

"Did you make a list of their household staff? Anyone of them also work for Winona?"

"Avril Birmingham works as a maid in both households," he said. "But she also works in at least five other households."

"But she could have taken the gun," I said.

"Yes." He finished his steak and took a sip of wine. "But I don't want you to contact her in any way," he said pointedly. "We don't know if she is dangerous or not."

"Okay," I said.

"Seriously."

I took my last bite of steak and chewed thoughtfully. "Seriously," I promised.

"Also, with Michelle here, you should put that murder board away. I don't want you to spook her."

"I think she's not easily spooked," I said. "But I'll put it away."

"Thanks." He stood, picked up our plates, and took them to the sink. "Thanks for dinner. I hate to eat and run, but—"

"You've got a murderer to catch," I said and gave him a kiss. "Be careful out there."

"I will," he said. "You stay safe." He hugged me tight and then put on his cap and walked out into the balmy night.

I sighed long and hard and started the dishes. Mal chewed on her bone in her dog bed in the living room and Mella sat on top of the wing-backed chair. "Well, kids, we're about to have more company."

Mal barked and wagged her little stump tail. Mella licked her paw. I finished wiping the dishes when there was a knock at my back door. I used the peephole to see that it was Michelle, and I opened the door. "Hello, welcome, come on in," I said and secured the door behind her. "This is my little apartment."

"It's cute," she said.

Mal jumped up on her and sniffed her.

"Mal, get down," I said and scooped her up. "Sorry. She knows better but I'm afraid I've gotten lax on my training."

"No problem," Michelle said as she stood in my kitchen with a suitcase in hand. "She's cute."

Mella jumped up on the countertop to get a good look at our new guest.

"I hope you're not allergic to cats."

"No," Michelle said. "I love cats."

"Wonderful," I said and put Mal down. "Well, quick tour. This is the kitchen and open living room." I walked her out into the living area. "The guest room is through here." She followed me. "You can put your suitcase on the suitcase holder in the closet. Feel free to use the dresser or closet if you want to hang anything."

"Great," she said and put her suitcase down.

"The bathroom is right behind the kitchen here." I waved toward the bath just down the hall. "And my bedroom is on the right, right beside the guest room."

"Well, isn't this cozy?" she said.

"Can I get you some tea? Coffee?"

"Water, please," she said. "I'm an early-to-bed kind of person."

"Certainly," I said. "I put clean sheets and blankets on the bed. Let me know if you need anything."

"I will," she replied.

I got her some water and took it to her. She had unpacked her things and was hanging up clothes in the closet.

"How long do you think I'll have to be here?" she asked.

"I'm not sure," I said. "But I'd like to think that Rex is closing in on this killer."

"Really? That's a relief," she said.

"Here's your water. If you're up to it, why not come out and join me. We can chat."

"I'd really rather get ready for bed," she said.

"Okay," I agreed. "I get up pretty early to make fudge. I'll take Mal with me, so she doesn't disturb you. Oh, and here's a key to my door. When you go out to work in the morning, please lock up. And if for some reason, you get up before me and go out, please reset the alarm. The number is on the key. I've got security cameras on each corner, so it will be safe for you to come and go from the outside or if you prefer, you can leave through the Mc-Murphy's main door. That door locks automatically behind you."

"Okay."

"Oh, and . . ." I held out my hand. "There's coffee in the coffee bar downstairs and I have hot and cold cereal for breakfast. They're in the cupboard on the right, right next to the cupboard that holds my bowls. The milk is in the fridge, of course."

"Got it," she said and took my key. "Good night."

"Good night," I said and left her to close her door. One thing was for certain, she was going to be a very different houseguest than Carol was.

Easy Chocolate Cake

Ingredients:
1 cup sugar
¾ cup plus 2 tablespoons flour
½ cup unsweetened cocoa powder
¾ teaspoon of baking powder
¾ teaspoon of baking soda
½ teaspoon of salt
1 egg
½ cup milk
¼ cup vegetable oil
1 teaspoon vanilla
½ cup boiling water

Directions:
Preheat oven to 350 degrees F. Grease and flour one 8x8-inch pan.

Stir dry ingredients together. Make a well in the center. Add egg, milk, oil, and vanilla and mix for 2 minutes. Stir in boiling water. Batter will be runny. Pour into pan and bake for 25–30 minutes until a cake tester comes out clean.

Let cool completely. Frost with your favorite frosting or simply sprinkle with powdered sugar and serve. Makes 1 cake.

Chapter 42

That night I lay awake far too long. Something tickled at the back of my brain, but I couldn't figure out what it was. I tossed and turned and finally got up to stare at the murder board. I added the Alpines' staff that I knew of. They had a gardener, two maids who came in three times a week to clean up, a secretary, and a chef. They all went up on the murder board as they all had access to the gun in the Alpines' home. I did have to wonder why they didn't keep it safe in a gun safe, but then I supposed most people didn't. I wondered if the Alpines had a rifle missing as well. Not that I could go out and ask that. I doubted even Rex could get an answer from them on that question.

There was still nothing tangible linking them to Winona's murder. After all, the murder weapon had been covered in dirt and most likely wiped clean. Ballistics was the only thing linking the gun I found to the murders. Also, why would the killer dump the handgun in the flowerpot and start shooting people with a rifle?

I sighed and laid back down on my bed. Mal and Mella curled up on either side of me. At least no remaining members of the committee were alone.

It was a bit strange to have Michelle in my home, as I barely knew her, and she seemed distant. I knew she worked in the bank during the day and since it was only two blocks away it was easy access for her.

There was a bump and a bang. I sat up and looked out my window. It was Michelle. She was going somewhere. I glanced at the clock it was 3 a.m. What was she doing going out this time of night?

Maybe she realized she'd left the iron on at home or something she needed for work. I know it would have bothered me if I thought of it in the middle of the night. Or maybe she was like me and just couldn't sleep. Sighing, I got up. If I wasn't going to sleep, the least I could do was get started on the day's fudge making.

"How was it having Michelle stay with you?" Jenn asked. She and I and Frances stood around the reception desk. It was eight-thirty a.m., and I was done with my batches of fudge and waiting until the ten a.m. fudge demonstration.

"Okay," I said. "She went somewhere at three this morning. I thought it strange, because she works at the bank, but I haven't seen her to ask about it."

"She has a key to your place, doesn't she?"

"Yes." I rubbed the kinks in my neck. "She's free to

come and go as she wishes. I just wondered what the heck was going on."

"I wouldn't worry about it," Frances said. "She might have had trouble sleeping and gone home to get something she forgot. It has to be safe from the killer that early in the morning."

"I would think so," I agreed.

"Ah, Mrs. Alonzo," Frances said as one of our guests walked out of the elevator. "How was your stay?"

"Wonderful," the older woman said.

Jenn and I went upstairs to the office to leave Frances to her checkout duties. She could call me if she needed me.

"How's the morning sickness?" I asked.

"I'm still on ginger tea and crackers," she said with a shake of her head. "They say this could go on for the first three months. At least I'm not horribly bedridden like some women."

"I don't want to think about how having children would change my schedule," I said. "Until they were older, I would have to make fudge in the daytime hours. I don't see me being able to get up at four a.m. and sneak off to work like I do now."

"I'm not concerned," Jenn said. "I'll just bring the baby to work with me. A carrier, a baby papoose sling, and I can keep working."

"If you want to," I said. "I hear it's exhausting."

"Oh, I'll want to," she said. "I never saw myself as a stay-at-home mom."

"It will be nice to have a baby around," I said. "They bring great energy to the McMurphy and I'm sure Mal will be a good babysitter. Right, Mal?"

"Arf."

"Shane is crazy about it," Jenn said. "He keeps wanting to wait on me hand and foot."

"Enjoy it," I said. "I hear things will get crazy once the baby is born."

"Speaking of the baby, we'll have a reveal at the baby's gender party. I thought on the rooftop deck."

"Sounds good to me," I said. "I'd love to plan it." I could already see the balloons and the cake and presents. "I'll get Crazy Cakes to make one with the colored candies in the middle. When you cut it, everyone will know."

"Well, you have some time to put it all together." She sat in her chair. "I'm seven or eight weeks and they can't determine sex until at least fourteen weeks, but more like eighteen weeks."

"So late October," I said. "Even better."

"I don't want to know until the reveal. I'll have the doctor let you know so you can order the cake," Jenn said. "That way we'll be as surprised as everyone else."

"Sounds great!" I said. "What's on the event agenda now?"

"I've got an intimate wedding with just the bride and groom and their parents. Then there's the Pellstons' twenty-fifth anniversary. They're going to fill the entire hotel with their guests next week."

"Wonderful." I sat and opened my computer. "Room sales are up this year even with the fifteen percent discount you offer groups."

"I know," Jenn said with pride in her voice. "I told you I'd be good for the McMurphy."

"I never doubted you," I said. "Not once."

* * *

Later that afternoon I was in the lobby helping Frances when Michelle came through the lobby door.

"Hi, roomie," she said cheerfully.

"Hi," I said. "Is your shift over at the bank?"

"Yes, I get to leave at three-thirty—banker's hours, you know. It's why I'm able to stay on top of all my committee work and keep my garden going."

"Oh, your garden," I said. "Do you want me to go with you when you go to weed and water? It's best to have company."

"Sure," Michelle said. "It can go a day or two, so how about tomorrow?"

"Sounds good," I said. "Tomorrow it is."

"Well, I'm going up to change, then watch some TV."

"What do you want for dinner?" I asked. "I can pick up something from Doud's and cook."

"Oh, don't bother," she said. "I had a good lunch and will just have a snack later."

"Okay," I said and watched her disappear up the stairs. "She certainly is the opposite of Carol."

"It's a nice thing you are doing," Frances said. "I'm glad you are both staying safe from the killer."

"Rex told me to put the murder board away," I said. "I left it out. She hasn't asked me about it and has barely been in the living area. She keeps to her room."

"How's the investigation going?" Frances asked.

"I'm not sure," I said as truthfully as I could. "He now suspects it might be one of the Alpines' staff, because the Alpines themselves claim not to have known the gun was missing."

"Did any of their staff have cause to hate Winona?" Frances wondered.

"Only one person worked for both ladies and that's Avril Birmingham. Rex is going to question her today, I think."

"I know Avril's mother, Rhonda," Frances said. "She works at the Teatime Tea shop. You should go speak to her."

"You know what—I will," I said. "Maybe she can shine some light in the matter."

"Just don't go off Main Street alone," Frances warned.

"I'll take Mal," I said and grabbed my pup's leash and halter. "Come on, Mal, let's go for a walk." I left out the front and blended into the busy traffic. The Teatime Tea shop was on the other side of Main Street, closer to the end. We walked briskly down to the shop and entered. Bells jangled on the door. I picked up Mal and smiled at the lady working the counter.

"Excuse me, I'm looking for Rhonda Birmingham." I put on my best friendly face and smiled at her.

"I'm Rhonda," she said. "We don't allow animals in the shop."

"I'm Allie McMurphy. Frances Devaney said I should talk to you. Do you have time for a beverage? I'm buying."

"Oh, honey, I work in a tea shop, so I don't need a beverage, but I do have a fifteen-minute break coming up. I'll meet you at the Beanery in five minutes."

"Thank you," I said and Mal and I left. We waited in front of the Beanery with a coffee. They had outdoor bistro tables and chairs and Mal sat in my lap and watched the people go by. Finally, Rhonda stopped by.

"Hi, Allie," she said and took a seat. "What can I do for you?"

"I got you a water and a muffin," I said and pushed the

food to her. "I was wondering about Avril. I understand she worked for Winona Higer and the Alpines."

"She does," Rhonda said. "Why?"

"Did she ever talk about disliking working for either?"

"She works for at least five families." Rhonda took a bite out of her muffin. "She was quite torn up about Winona. She said that while she was difficult to please, she was a good tipper and now Avril has to find another family to work with to keep up her paycheck."

"Wait, she wasn't angry with Winona?"

"Not that I know of, no," Rhonda said and checked her watch. "But you can ask her yourself. She's home right now. She is staying at the Maple Manor Apartments, apartment A."

"Thanks!"

"It would be even better if you could offer her a job. I hear you run the McMurphy hotel."

"I do," I said. "And I might just be in need of an extra maid." I stood and put Mal down. "Thanks for taking your break with me."

"Thanks for the muffin," she said.

Mal and I headed toward the pink apartment building. It was on the far end of Main Street, past St. Anne's church. So technically it was Main Street as far as I was concerned. Therefore, it was safe to walk alone.

I knocked on the door. Avril answered. "Yes?"

"Avril Birmingham?"

"Yes." She was a small woman, slight of figure, wearing a T-shirt and a pair of high-waisted shorts.

"I'm Allie McMurphy," I said. "Your mom said I should come and talk with you."

"About what?"

"Can I come in?" Mal wagged her stump tail as if to say "please."

"Sure," Avril said and opened the door.

We stepped into a neat little room that was barely big enough for a love seat and a television. "Thanks. I understand you worked for Mrs. Higer."

"I did," she said. "Please have a seat." She waved toward the love seat and we sat together. Mal jumped up on my lap and extended a paw. "Oh, how sweet." Avril shook Mal's paw.

"I was wondering if you might know who would want to kill Mrs. Higer."

"Well, most anyone who met her." Avril sat back. "She was a terrible stickler and not nice about it."

"But you worked for her," I said. "If she was that bad, why did you stay?"

"She tipped very well," Avril said. "I'm going to miss working for her. She was a tough old biddy, but the money made it worth it."

"Listen, I'm in need of a backup maid when the McMurphy is making a quick transition," I said. "Would you be interested?"

"Gosh, yes," she said. "I work in the afternoons for other families, but you can have my mornings as early as six-thirty."

"That's great." I shifted in my seat. "I'll have my friend Jenn give you a call whenever we need an extra pair of hands."

"Thank you," she said. "You won't regret it."

"May I use your restroom?" I asked.

"Certainly," she said. "It's through the kitchen, the second door on the right. I'd be happy to watch your dog if you want."

"Thanks," I said and gave her Mal's leash. I stepped into the tiny kitchen. It was compact and neat. There was a small table and two chairs snugged up against the window. She had a small back porch that was screened in and opened to the street. Out of curiosity I looked out and noted her shelves filled with canning jars and vases. There in the corner stood a rifle. It seemed out of place with the flower vases and frilly, labeled jelly jars.

I hurried to the bathroom and washed my hands. Avril might not admit to having it out for Winona, but she did have access to both a handgun and a rifle. I needed to get out of here and contact Rex.

"You have a lovely place," I said as I came out of the kitchen. Avril was playing tug with Mal and her leash.

"Thanks," she said and stood. "And thanks for offering the extra work. I sure could use it."

"My pleasure." I took Mal's leash and went to the front door. Then I turned back to Avril. "Do you know Natasha Alpine?"

"Of course, I've cleaned their home for two summers in a row."

"Did you know she won a sharpshooter competition?" I asked.

"I did," Avril said. "I came in second."

"That's amazing," I said. "I've never owned a gun, let alone done any target practice. I'm afraid I'd be a bad shot."

"It's easy, really, once you've made up your mind to pull the trigger," she advised. "You should go out to the shooting range. You might find it therapeutic."

"I'll think about that," I said with a forced chuckle. "Come on, Mal, let's go home."

I hurried Mal out of the apartment house and down the

street. When I got a safe distance down Main Street and was surrounded by people, I called Rex.

"Manning," he answered.

"Rex, I just came from Avril Birmingham's apartment. I saw a rifle on her back porch, and she said she came in second in the sharpshooter contest, just under Natasha."

"Allie, slow down," he advised. "Take a breath and tell me what you really mean."

"I think Avril is our killer."

Chapter 43

"Avril has means and motive," I said to Rex over dinner. "Did you get a chance to question her? Did you see the rifle on her back porch?"

"I went over there," he said. "She had no idea what I was talking about and when I asked if I could do a light search of her house, she told me to get a warrant."

"But I saw a rifle," I said. "I don't know what kind it was. Maybe a thirty-ought-six? She also had access to the automatic handgun at the Alpines. It has to be her."

"Well, until you can put her in silver fairy wings and get her fingerprints on the rifle and prove the rifle is a ballistics match, we don't have a case. Besides, her motive is weak. Why work for someone for two summers and then snap and kill them? Especially when she claims that Winona was a big tipper."

"I've got the photos," I said. "I'm going to go back

over them and prove Avril was at the bonfire. Will that give you enough to get a warrant?"

"It depends on the judge," he said. "It would be better if I had a bullet from that rifle to match with ballistics, or at the very least, a matching fingerprint on the gun. But like I said, the handgun was wiped clean and until I get a warrant, I can't check that rifle."

The back door opened and Michelle walked in. "Hi guys," she said. "Don't mind me, I'm going to bed."

"I have enough dinner to fix you a plate," I offered.

"No thanks," she said and yawned. "Like I said, I'm off to bed." She walked through the living room and into the guest room and gently closed the door.

"Don't say anything to Michelle about this," Rex said. "No need to spread rumors and get a witch hunt going."

"All right," I agreed. "Let me know when you get that warrant. I think you'll find the rifle that hit Amy in Avril's house."

The next morning, after my ten a.m. demonstration, Carol came running into the hotel. "Allie, did you hear the news?"

"What news?" I asked.

"They got a warrant to search Avril Birmingham's house and took a rifle, among other things. And I hear they did a ballistics check, and that rifle matches the gun that shot Amy and Elias."

"Oh, that's good news," I said. "As long as Avril's in custody."

"She is," Carol said. "But I thought you and I could go over the bonfire pictures to see if we can't place her at the bonfire that night."

"Well, I'm free now," I said and took off my chef's coat and hat. "Let's go look."

We went upstairs and Mal followed. The apartment was quiet and the guest room closed. "Can I get you some coffee?" I asked. "I've got coffee cake, too."

"You do?"

"Yes, I learned from the best," I said and winked at her.

"Then yes, I do want some, thanks."

"First, I'll go get the pictures." I went into my room and grabbed the envelope where I'd stored the photos. I glanced at the murder board and saw that Avril's picture was drooping. I unpinned it and stuck it back up. Killer caught!

"Okay, let's lay these out and look for Avril," I said. "Remember, she doesn't have to have silver wings, but it would be nice if she did."

"Okay, let me at them," Carol said and dumped the photos out of the envelope and onto the counter while I poured coffees and cut two pieces of coffee cake.

We sat in comfortable silence looking through the photos when Mal jumped down and ran to the guest room door. Michelle came out.

"Goodness, I must have overslept," she said, yawned, and poured herself a cup of coffee. "Lucky for me I took the day off from work. You know, a mental health day. I needed it, considering all we've been going through. What are you two doing?"

"Looking for pictures of Avril Birmingham at the bonfires," Carol said. "They arrested her today. It turns out the rifle in her home matched the gun that killed Elias. So now we're trying to help tie her to the other murders as well."

"Really? She had the rifle?" Michelle said. "But a handgun killed Winona."

"That gun belonged to the Alpines," I said. "Avril had access to it because she was a maid in the Alpine home."

"Wow, so, it's safe to say I can go home today?" Michelle sipped her coffee.

"Yes," I said. "If you hang on, I can help you take your stuff back."

"Oh, no need," she said. "I only brought the one suitcase. I'll be out of your hair by the time you finish your afternoon demonstration." She paused. "Oh, look here, it's Avril." She pulled out a photo with Avril dressed as a harlequin with light blue fairy wings.

"Look, blue fairy wings. Could be mistaken for silver in the moonlight," I said.

"True," Carol said. "But her costume is quite snug. Where would she hide a gun?"

"Huh," I picked up the photo. "Again, we have to ask, why would you bring a gun to the bonfire. I mean, we truly think Winona's murder wasn't calculated. Why did she steal a gun and then bring it to the bonfire, unless she preplanned the act?"

"So maybe it wasn't a spur-of-the-moment event," Michelle said as she came out of the guest bedroom with her suitcase. "It seems that you were wrong to think it was."

"That's the answer, then," Carol said. "Maybe we had the crime-of-passion thing wrong. It certainly fits the murders."

"Well, I'll take this picture to Rex," I said. "It might help him build his case."

"I'm off." Michelle gave me a hug. "Thanks for letting me stay here."

"You're welcome," I said. "Anytime. And don't tell anyone about the pictures, please. Rex said to leave you out of my investigation."

She pretended to lock her mouth and throw away the key. "Mum's the word."

"Oh, one more thing," I said and held out my hand. "Key, please."

"Oh, yes, I almost forgot." She pulled it out of her pocket and handed it to me. "Thanks for solving this and letting me get my life back."

"We all got our lives back," Carol said. "Isn't it wonderful?"

Chapter 44

"I'm off to see Michelle," I told Frances.

"Didn't she just leave this morning?" Frances asked.

"I found a pair of shoes she missed when I was stripping the bed. Since Rex has the killer in custody, it's safe for Mal and me to walk to Michelle's and return them."

"I agree," Frances said. "I'll hold down the fort until you get back."

"Thanks! It shouldn't take much more than an hour or so."

Mal and I went out the back door. My pup had a favorite potty spot and I waited for her to go when I spotted Mr. Beecher coming down the alley.

"Hello, Allie," he said. Mal raced toward him for the treat in his pocket. "How's the murder investigation going?"

"Rex has the killer in custody," I said. "Avril Birming-

ham had access to the handgun that killed Winona and
she had the rifle that killed Elias in her house."

"That was convenient," he said. "I thought she was a
sweet girl. I ran into her on occasion on my walks and she
was always so cheerful."

"She had means," I said. "Motive is a little sketchy.
But everyone knows that Winona was a difficult person
to work for. Michelle can testify to that."

"You're free to safely walk," he said and handed Mal
another treat.

"Yes," I said. "Michelle left a pair of shoes under the
bed, so we're going to go return them."

"Enjoy," he said.

The day was warm and sunny. The smell of fudge and
popcorn filled the air. The sounds of birds and people
laughing lifted my heart. Mackinac Island was a wonder-
land of state parks and old-time fun when there wasn't a
killer on the loose.

We arrived at Michelle's and I knocked on the door.
"Hello? Michelle?"

She didn't answer, so I thought I'd go around back.
The shed door was open, so I went that way. "Michelle?"
I called. I found her in the shed, filling a wheelbarrow
with bags of soil.

"Allie, what's up?" she asked as Mal and I stepped inside.

"You left a pair of shoes under the bed," I said and
lifted the bag I'd put the shoes in.

"Oh, my goodness," she said and straightened with a
rake in her hand. "Thanks for bringing them."

"No problem," I said. Mal sniffed around and poked
her nose at something on a bottom shelf. "Mal, come
here," I said and bent to pick her up. She had poked a

bottle of weed killer. "Oh, no," I said. "That's poison." I straightened. "Wait, why do you have weed killer? I thought you were an organic gardener?"

Michelle swung the rake, a pain exploded in my temple, and everything went black.

I woke up in a cool basement with my hands and feet tied. Mal was in a cage beside me. "What happened?" My head pounded and then I remembered: Michelle had weed killer. The very thing that could kill roses. So, she was the one who destroyed Winona's roses. But why tie me up? Why knock me in the head?

The door to the basement opened and a light came on. I blinked against the brightness, my head hurting worse.

"Hello?" I said, my voice croaking from dryness. How long had I been out?

"You're awake," I heard Michelle say.

"Michelle? Why am I tied up? What's going on?"

"You saw the weed killer," she said. "You weren't supposed to see that."

"Was it you that killed Winona's prizewinning roses? Why?"

"She never acknowledged me. She used me, used my ideas, told everyone they were hers. I was sick of it. Sick. Do you know what it's like to work for a person for five years, and they still don't see you? To love someone and they still don't see you? To do everything for someone, sacrifice your entire life for someone, and have them not even acknowledge you?"

"That must have been terrible," I said. "You loved her? Winona?"

"I did," she said. "Why do you think I did everything

for her, but she never saw me. She never asked how I was or what I thought. If I did give her an idea, she would take it and run with it as if it were her own. You should have seen how everyone was fawning all over her about the festival. What a great job she did. What a wonderful idea it was. But the idea was mine. The work, all that work was mine. All I asked for was for her to see me. To acknowledge me for a moment. To be proud of me. To thank me."

"Michelle . . ." I swallowed. "Was Winona your mother?"

"I wish she was," Michelle said. "I've worked for her since I was sixteen. I admired her, worshipped her. But she took me for granted. There's only so much a person can take."

"What happened the night of the bonfire?"

"She refused to acknowledge me. She let me stand there beside her while she took all the credit . . . again. I finally snapped. We argued. I told her how I felt. How I'd had enough. She laughed. She laughed at me and said I was being ridiculous. So, then I told her about the roses, and she got mad. But I didn't care. I wanted her to beg."

"Michelle, where did you get the gun?"

"I took it from the Alpines a few weeks before. Just to see if anyone would notice. They are all so self-involved. They never did notice. I could go into their home and steal them blind, and they would never suspect me. No one suspected me."

"You had the gun with you at the bonfire?"

"No, after we argued I went home and got it. She was so sure of herself. She fired me, me! After all I did. So, I fired back."

"You killed Winona."

She laughed. "Yes, of course. She dropped into the

water and I left. No one cared. No one noticed me. I got away with murder."

"But what about Patricia?"

"That nosy busybody had to say she saw someone with silver wings." Michelle paced in front of me. "She was so proud of seeing it. She went to you and told you. She was about to tell Rex. I couldn't have that."

"You shot her," I said. "And dumped her in the bushes."

"No one was supposed to find her, but then you and your little dog had to come along. I barely escaped in time."

"I don't understand," I said. "You threatened Carol."

"I wanted to draw attention off of me. If you thought the committee was at risk and I was on the committee, then you wouldn't suspect me."

"I didn't," I said. "I let you stay at my house."

"I knew about your stupid murder board. You were so far off. It made me happy. You and Rex kept going back to the Alpines, so I hid the gun where you would find it. The gun that belonged to them. They deserved to go to jail. They are cruel and barely acknowledge their help."

"And they saw you as the help."

"Why not, it's how Winona treated me."

"But why shoot Amy?"

"Rex wasn't taking the Alpines into custody. I even gave him the murder weapon, so I had to raise the stakes. I had to make it seem like the killer was targeting the committee. I broke into her home, but that wasn't enough. So I shot her, but I didn't kill her. I like her. She was a calculated risk."

"Where did you get the rifle?"

"It belonged to my grandfather," she said. "I was in the

same shooting competition as Natasha, not that anyone remembered. Sometimes it's best no one notices you."

"And Elias?"

"That man—" She stopped pacing and looked at me. "He figured out I hurt the roses. He should have just kept his mouth shut. He should have just let it go after Winona was killed. But no, he came to me and confronted me. I was afraid he'd figure out the rest."

"And you killed him for it," I said, my heart pounding in my chest. I knew where this confession was going. All I could do was keep talking and hope Rex would come find me. Had I told anyone where I was going? Had I told Frances? Would she come looking for me? Wait, yes. Frances knew. That meant there was hope.

"When I saw you were looking for a rifle, I had to get rid of it."

"You left my place at three in the morning and planted the gun on Avril's back porch. How did she not notice it?"

"Who really looks closely at the things on their back porch? I placed it near the brooms and mops. Even if she had found it, her prints would have been on it. She would have to explain it. It worked, didn't it? Didn't you and Rex blame her? Didn't she get arrested?"

"So why hurt me? I mean, you got away with it. Why?"

"That darned weed killer. I knew you would figure it out once you realized I had poisoned the roses. I should have gotten rid of it, but I thought I was in the clear."

"You would have been if you hadn't left a pair of shoes under the guest room bed," I said. "If you had been in your house and not the shed."

"I really don't want to kill you, Allie," she said. "But I've come this far. Too far to stop now."

"But if you were going to kill me, why didn't you when you knocked me out?"

"I guess I wanted someone to know what I'd done. I wanted someone to see me and think how clever I was. So clever you didn't even know it was me or you would have never invited me to stay with you."

"Yes," I said and swallowed hard. "You are very clever. I didn't suspect you, but if you kill me now, Rex will know that Avril is the wrong suspect, and all your hard work would have been for nothing."

"Right, so right," she said. "It means I'm going to have to be even more clever. It's why I've brought you to this basement. You see, if I just make you disappear, no one will know."

"How are you going to do that? I told Frances I was coming here to bring you back your shoes. Someone will check."

"You think we're at my house? How quaint. Oh, don't worry, Rex already came by my house while you were sleeping. I told him you dropped off my shoes and left. I thought you were heading to the senior center, but I didn't know for sure." She loomed over me. "He left and didn't even look back."

"Are you going to leave me in your basement?"

"Like I said, it's not my basement." She smiled. "They'll never find you. They say it takes three days without water and a week without food to kill a person," she said. "I've always wondered if it's true."

My body shook as I swallowed hard again. "Surely, they will come here, wherever *here* is," I pointed out. "Isn't it better to take me somewhere off the island?" If I could convince her to move me, then I had a chance of leaving some kind of a trail. I don't know what, but I'd think of something.

"You would prefer I kill you fast," she said. "Too bad my guns are all gone. I suppose poison would do the trick . . ."

"No, no," I said. "I'll starve. I don't mind starving."

"I'm going to put you in the utility closet," she said. "You can scream all you like in there, no one will hear you. The window has been bricked off for years and no one will look for you here."

"Where is *here*?"

"That's for me to know and you not to care."

She came over and grabbed me under the arms. I twisted and fought as best I could with my hands and feet tied, but she was strong. Really strong.

"I will hit you with the shovel this time if you don't stop fighting. Who knows, maybe the next whack or two or three will solve this problem for me."

I went still as she dragged me into the four-by-eight-foot utility closet in the basement. Then locked the door. It was very dark, giving testament to the truth in her saying she bricked off the window. I heard her dragging stuff in front of the door. No one would think to look for me here.

My heart sank.

Was I going to die a slow death?

Chapter 45

My eyes adjusted slowly to the dark. The room was made of old stone and mortar. There was a water heater and a furnace in the room with me and Mal. It meant it was warm and musty. I'd been in a basement situation before. Why did people keep trying to lock me in their basements? I was beginning to really hate basements.

But I'd gotten out of the last one. I could get out of this one, too. All I needed was to get untied. My hands were behind my back. She had used thick and sturdy rope and I couldn't slide my hands out of the loops. Maybe there was a sharp edge to a rock on the wall. I stood and leaned against it and ran my fingers along the wall looking for anything I could rub the ropes against.

It seemed like hours before I found a dull edge. But it

was an edge and if she was right, I might have seven days to rub the ropes apart. I'd better get started.

I worked the ropes for what seemed like forever, my wrists raw. I was exhausted and crying as I slid down the wall to sit on the cold floor. What light there was came from the bottom of the door. I inched my way over to the door to see if I could see anything. There were boxes in the way. But the bottom of the door was wood. Maybe I could rub the ropes on it. I rolled so my back was to the door and worked some more. The pain of my wrist was nearly unbearable. I could feel blood running down, but I kept sawing until I felt it give. It spurred me on as I pulled against it and it gave some more.

Finally, finally my hands were free. My shoulders ached as I sat up against the wall. I untied the ropes and pulled them off me. Then I tore strips off of my shirt and wrapped them around my wrists. There was no water to clean the wounds, so the shirt would have to do.

Working the tight knots around my ankles, I finally freed myself of the ropes and, exhausted, I sat down and closed my eyes.

I woke up thirsty and my head pounded. I felt a knot on the side of my head where she had struck me. Was it the day before? Who knows if it had only been a day? I lay back down on the floor to see if I could tell if it was day or night from the basement windows. But the boxes were in the way. I stuck my fingers under the door, scraping my hands and pushed on the bottom of the boxes, but they were heavy.

That was a wash. I carefully felt around until I found Mal's cage and let her out. She jumped up on me and licked my face. I squeezed her until she squeaked in protest. Having Mal with me helped boost my morale. I began to wonder if I could dig the mortar out of the bricked-off window. Standing, I put Mal down and I felt around the upper walls until I came to a hole in the top of the wall. The window was above my head. Darn it.

I sat down and cried again. Mal sat in my lap, pawing at my hands and licking my face as if to say everything will be all right. Exhausted and afraid, I took a deep breath. Michelle, the killer was Michelle, and I hadn't even realized it. I'd been in the shed before, but too briefly to notice the weed killer. No wonder she'd asked me what I was doing.

She'd been in my home. She'd looked at my murder board. Carol and I had looked at pictures, looking for the killer, while she stood right there. She must have been so pleased with herself.

I sighed and told myself to buck up.

The rock wall might be climbable. People rock climbed all the time, right? Maybe if I found some handholds and footholds, I could work my way up to the window. I fell three times before I managed to get high enough to brace my legs against the wall and reach the mortar in the window. The bricks were really in there tight, not letting in any light. But I used my fingers to dig at the mortar. To no avail. I might get a length of wood off the bottom of the door, I thought. I shimmied down the wall, ran to the door, and spent my time digging at the soft wood until I managed to get a half-inch-wide three-inch-long piece of wood. If nothing else, I could stab Michelle with it, if she came back.

Unfortunately, I was pretty sure she wasn't coming back. Exhausted, I sat down and rested again, falling asleep with Mal in my lap. I had no way to track time; I only felt my thirst and my hunger. I climbed back up the wall and banged away at the mortar with the stick until it began to crumble. Heartened, I created a hole and saw that it looked like daytime. But what day? Hopefully, Rex was trying to find me. Hopefully, he'd come back to Michelle's and question her again.

I kept digging at that hole until it was dime-sized, then quarter-sized, then the side of a brick was exposed. I wondered where Michelle was. Could I call out from my hole and be heard?

What was going on?

I wiggled and wiggled the brick until darkness fell and my back screamed with stiffness and pain. But I got it free. A few bangs of the stick on the mortar and the brick above it was loose. I worked through the darkness until I had a hole the size of my head. Could I possibly slip out? At best, I could put Mal through the hole and set her free. She could find Rex and bring him to me.

I spent another unknown amount of time digging at a third and fourth brick, making the hole big enough for Mal. Climbing down, I called my pup to me.

"Here, Mal!" I picked her up, climbed as best I could with her under my arm, and hung by my fingertips while I shoved her out of the hole in the bricks. "Go get Rex. Mal, go get Rex."

She scurried off as I noted the window was hidden behind a bush. I spent time wiggling out more blocks until I could reach out and grab the base of the bush and tucked my head and shoulders out. But would my hips fit? I was stuck halfway in the dark. Great. With my luck, Rex would find me stuck. I had to trust Mal was getting him, even though it was dark out. She would either return home or sniff him out.

Instead of worrying, I turned back to wiggling yet another brick out while my feet hung in the air. There simply wasn't any purchase to push myself through.

Finally, after what seemed like forever, I could hear a bark in the distance. Good Mal! I wriggled even harder, scraping myself up good until I was free.

Laying on the cool ground, out of breath, I was shocked I'd managed to free myself. Now all I had to do was get to freedom without Michelle knowing.

I held my breath, but heard no one outside, so I army-crawled out of the bushes. Too tired to run, I half crawled, half crouched along the side of the building. There was a fence and a gate. I still didn't know exactly where I was, but the barking was closer.

A glance back at the building showed no lights were on. Managing to pull myself up, I unlocked the gate and stumbled onto the street. Falling again, I felt like a girl in a horror show. Get up, get up, get up. I kept going until I was down the block and around the corner.

Michelle had taken my cell phone. I had no key to get back into the McMurphy. The police station seemed so far away, but I kept going until I couldn't and curled up against a fence and closed my eyes.

"Allie, Allie, wake up," I heard Rex call to me. I felt licking on my face and I opened my eyes and sat up. "What happened? Where have you been?" he asked.

"Michelle," I said and closed my eyes against the exhaustion. "It was Michelle."

Chapter 46

I woke up and it was daylight. Rex sat beside me, holding my hand. The clinic room was cool and an IV was
in my arm. "Rex," I said through a dry mouth.

"Shush," he said, standing. "Let me get you some water."
Pouring water from a pitcher beside the bed, he filled a
cup half full and brought it to me. Then he helped me sit
up so I could take a sip.

"Michelle," I said as I laid back against the pillow.
"She killed everyone. She confessed everything to me."

"Charles brought her in for questioning," he said. "She
said she has no idea why you said her name except you
want to keep her safe."

"No, no, she locked me in a basement. What day is it?
What time? Where's Mal?"

"Mal helped us find you. She showed up at the police
station and wouldn't stay still until we followed her," he

said. "She took us straight to you. You've been gone three nights," he informed me. "You are dehydrated, but otherwise in relatively good shape. There are contusions around your wrists, ankles and scrapes and cuts on your hands and body. We had to document them all."

His brilliant blue eyes gazed at me with such fierceness. "If I weren't a lawman, I'd have to kill whoever did this to you."

"It was Michelle Bell," I said again, then closed my eyes against the exhaustion. "She confessed everything to me."

I woke up again when the doctor came in. "You are a very lucky woman," he said. "You were severely dehydrated. It wouldn't have been long if you hadn't escaped."

"She told me three days without water and seven without food. Is that true?"

"Yes," he said. "Give or take. It depends on the body."

"I've brought you some food," the nurse said, bringing in a tray of eggs and toast that made my mouth water.

"Looks yummy," I said.

"We'll start you off with small, simple meals for the next day," he said. "To get your body used to eating."

"When can she go home?" Rex asked, entering the room.

"Later this afternoon, once the IV is done," the doctor said.

The nurse checked my IV as I scooped up a forkful of scrambled eggs and tasted the delicious warmth of egg and salt.

Rex waited until the doctor and nurse left and I'd eaten a couple of bites. "We have Michelle in custody."

"Oh, good," I said. "Did you find the window that I crawled out of?"

"We did," he said. "What were you doing at the Garrets' house?"

"The Garrets? Do I know them?"

"I doubt it," he said. "They're in Europe and won't be on the island this summer."

"Michelle must have had a key," I said. "She must have been looking after the place. She knew it quite well. Well enough to lock me in with a bricked-over window."

"I have no idea how you got out of that small hole," Rex said.

"By sheer determination," I said. "I didn't have my cell phone and I was afraid to call out in case she heard me."

"I understand," he said and took my hand. "Allie, tell me what happened from the beginning."

I went over everything, from seeing the weed killer to waking up in the basement. "She told me everything," I said. "Winona was killed out of anger and passion, but the rest she wanted to shut up before we figured out it was her."

"She planted the rifle in Avril's home?"

"Avril is known for leaving her back porch open. She wouldn't have gone looking for a rifle." I ate another bite of egg before I felt too full to continue.

"Right now, I'm holding her for kidnaping, assault, and attempted murder," he said. "We've got a warrant to go through her home and property with a fine-tooth comb. But I have no evidence linking her to her confession and unless I can get her to confess, then there's no way to tie her to the murders. It's a she said/she said situation."

"But you let Avril go, right?"

"She's out on bail until we can sort things out," he said.

I frowned at him. "You do believe me, right?"

"Yes, I believe you," he said. "I will always believe you. There's just procedures and evidence that we need for an airtight case."

I frowned at him. "Let me question her," I said. "I can get your confession."

"That's highly irregular," he pointed out. "Let us search her place first."

"Okay," I said with a sigh.

"Allie, how are you feeling?" Frances asked as she and Douglas and Jenn came through the door one at a time.

"You nearly scared us half to death," Jenn said.

"You shouldn't have gone over there alone," Douglas chided.

"Guys, guys, I'm okay," I said. "I'm safe."

Mal barked and jumped up on the bed to lick my face.

"No dogs in the clinic," the nurse chided from the other side of the door.

I handed Mal to Frances. "I get to go home in a few hours. I'm so looking forward to being home."

"Can you tell us what happened?" Jenn asked.

There was a knock at the door. It was Liz. "Do you have any words for the paper?" she asked.

"I'm fine," I teased her.

"Right, how are you doing?" she asked.

"I've been better," I said.

"I think her statement can wait," Rex said, his tone protective.

"I'll give you a statement tomorrow, if that's okay." I shifted in the bed to sit up better. "I might have more information for you then."

"That's fine," she said. "I guess I was a little too aggressive. Really, I'm glad you are safe."

"It's just dehydration and a few scrapes and bruises," I said.

"We were all so worried," Frances said. "But we'll get out of here and let you rest. Besides, I have to take Mal." She moved to the bed, leaned over, and gave me a kiss on the cheek. "I'll call your mom. She was on her way here."

"Oh, no—yes, please tell Mom and Dad I'm fine and I'll video chat them tonight to prove it."

"I will." She straightened. "Come on, Douglas, let's go take care of the McMurphy. I'm sure the fudge customers miss you, Allie."

"I'll see you tonight." But first I was going to convince Rex to let me grill Michelle. I know she can't lie to me. Not after her explanation in the basement. This time she's going to be seen.

Chapter 47

"Are you sure you're up to this?" Rex asked.

"I'm sure," I said. I'd gone home and showered and put on clean clothes. It felt good and I almost felt like myself. "I'll get a confession out of her. Or I will stay there until I do."

"I'm going in with you," he said. "So, you'll be safe."

"Got it." I rolled my head as if preparing for a fight. "Let's do this."

We walked into the interrogation room. "Hello, Allie," Michelle said. She seemed calmer than she did when I last saw her. But I felt like her desperation was just under the surface.

"Hello, Michelle," I said and sat across from her.

"We found weed killer in your home," Rex said. "Allie tells me you were the one to poison Winona's roses. Why did you do that?"

Michelle looked from one of us to the other for a moment. "I'm not going to admit to destruction of property."

"She didn't notice you at all, did she?" I said with sympathy. "She treated you like a piece of work equipment and you had been her trusty helper for nearly eighteen years. Weren't you?"

"I worked hard for her." Michelle's calm slipped a little.

"She was harsh with everyone who worked for her," I said. "But you most of all. She still treated you like a child. Didn't she? She took your ideas and said they were hers."

"How did it feel to see her get all the congratulations at the festival?" Rex asked. "I saw Winona that night. She practically glowed from all the positive comments."

"We know the festival idea was yours," I said. "That you did a majority of the work while she took all the glory."

"So?"

"So that had to make you angry," Rex said. He pushed a newspaper article in front of her. In it, the committee and especially Winona were praised. "They interviewed her and she never mentioned you, did she?" He pushed another interview toward her. This one praised local volunteer, Winona Higer. "She boasted she had done a majority of the work."

"I would have been angry with her over that," I said. "Were you?"

"Maybe," Michelle said, her calm slipping further.

"Don't you think it should have been you who was praised for the work you did?" Rex pushed a third article toward her. "Don't you think she should have at least mentioned you in her articles? That it was your idea?"

"She was terrible not to even bring up your name," I agreed. "I don't know how you didn't say anything. I would have had it out with her. I mean, there's a point where it makes sense to put your foot down. Is that what you did the night of the bonfire? Did you put your foot down and stand up for yourself?"

"I did," she said. "And that woman was awful. She laughed at me. Laughed and said I couldn't handle the responsibility she took for everything. That I just thought it was my idea when it was actually all hers."

"What happened then?" I asked softly. "I mean, I would have wanted to hit her for laughing at me."

"Is that when you got the gun?" Rex asked. "Is that when you came back and shot her?"

"She fired you, didn't she? It's understandable if you were in a rage," I said. "I would have been."

"I was furious," she admitted. "Something snapped in me and I did get the gun."

"And you shot her, didn't you?" I said. "Rex is looking at you now. Everybody sees you. Don't you want people to know what you did and why you did it? Come on—it will be a relief to tell your story again. Didn't it feel better after you told me the first time?"

"Fine, I shot her. Are you happy now?" Tears poured down her cheeks and I reached for a box of tissues and handed them to her. She blew her nose. "I don't remember shooting her. I was so angry, but I remember seeing her fall into the water. I was horrified," she whispered. "This woman I'd loved over half my life was dead."

"And Patricia, Amy, and Elias?"

"I had to silence them, I had to get you to look the other way," she said. "They were too close to figuring me out."

"Like me," I said.

"Like you." She looked at me, her eyes once again defiant. "This is all your fault. If you had only let it go, I would be free and Avril in jail."

"Avril is innocent, isn't she?" Rex asked.

"Of course she is, you stupid cop. It's so easy to fool you. If Allie hadn't been on to me, I would have gotten away with everything."

"*Everything* meaning killing three people and wounding another?" Rex asked.

"Yes," she shouted. "Of course. Everything."

I swallowed hard at the angry energy she exuded. "Excuse me," I said as my heart raced, and I felt panic building inside me. I got up and shakily opened the door and leaned against the wall, taking big gulps of air.

Rex followed. "Are you okay?" he asked gently.

"No," I said. "I think I'm having a panic attack."

"That's reasonable, considering all you went through," he said. "Come on, I'll take you home." He put his arm around me and signaled for another officer to look after Michelle. I leaned on him and when we stepped out into the cooling dusk, I took a deep breath. "That was harder than I thought."

"You did a great job," he said.

"Will she be charged now?"

"She will," he said, walking beside me. "We have her confession on tape."

"I'm glad she didn't ask for a lawyer," I said.

"She was arrogant and thought she didn't need one."

"*Arrogant* is only the beginning of what's wrong with Michelle." I took Rex's hand in mine as we walked. "I'm glad it's over."

"Me too, Allie. Me too."

Chapter 48

The next day I felt as if I'd been hit by a truck. I guess the adrenaline of escaping had made it so I didn't notice how I had to twist my body to pull myself out of the window. I'd made my morning fudge and Frances had told me to go up and take a bath to ease my muscles. I didn't disagree. When I got out, I put on a sundress and sandals and went downstairs, where Frances, Douglas, Jenn, Shane, Rex, and Liz were gathered around the reception desk.

"Did I miss the party invitation?" I asked.

"Allie, how are you feeling?" Jenn asked.

"I hurt in places I didn't know could hurt," I said. "But I'm fine."

"Rex tells us you got Michelle to confess," Liz said. "That's a great story. Can I get an exclusive?"

I laughed. "I don't think anyone else is interested, so sure."

"You'd be surprised," she said. "This will go out on the wire and others will pick it up. Local girl escapes from serial murderer. Meaning she killed more than one, not that she was a serial killer," Liz clarified. "Serial killers generally don't have motives."

"Potato, potahto," Frances said. "Michelle was messed up."

"She snapped," I agreed. "It's hard to take daily abuse and harder yet to stand up to it and then get laughed at. I think we all could have snapped, given the circumstances."

"I'm certainly glad this is over," Jenn said.

"Speaking of news," I said to Jenn and Shane. "Did you tell everyone yours?"

They both grinned wide. "In case you didn't already know, we're pregnant!"

"Congrats, again!" Frances said and gave her a hug. "I'm so happy for you."

"Congratulations," Douglas said.

"That's great news," Rex said.

"We're going to have a reveal party," I said. "When they find out the sex, we'll have a big celebration."

"It will be nice to have children around the McMurphy on a full-time basis again," Frances said.

"What about you two?" Douglas asked.

I felt the heat of a blush rush up my cheeks. "Rex and me? We're just dating." I glanced at him. "I mean, we just started dating. We're certainly a long way away from babies."

"I don't know," Rex said. "It might be nice to have a little Allie running around solving crimes."

"Well, I certainly hope not until she's at least eighteen," Frances said. "My heart can't take another family member always getting into danger."

"You want kids?" I studied Rex's handsome face.

"Sure," he said sincerely. "At least two. Don't you?"

"I guess with everything going on, I'd not thought about it," I said. "But yeah, I'd like to have kids one day."

Rex's eyes twinkled. "Nice to know we're on the same page."

"Well, for now, let's celebrate Jenn and Shane. I have a nice bottle of sparkling wine and a bottle of sparkling water in my apartment."

"It's brunch time," Frances said.

"Then I've also got orange juice. Let's make some mimosas."

"Allie is always prepared," Jenn said with a laugh.

"I'm just happy to have everyone here." I led them up the stairs.

"We're happy you're back where you belong and only a little worse for wear," Frances said.

Another adventure in my life, I thought. Next time I hope it's a little less deadly.

Acknowledgments

A special thank-you goes out to the folks of Mackinac Island who answer my questions and let me embellish the truth. No book is made in a vacuum. So special thanks to my awesome agent, Paige Wheeler, and my wonderful editor, Michaela Hamilton. And all the wonderful people at Kensington Books who work tirelessly to give you the best books possible.

Extra fun for fans of Nancy Coco's cozy mysteries!
Don't miss her new Oregon Honeycomb series.
Keep reading to enjoy the opening pages of *A Matter of
Hive and Death*, featuring honey store owner Wren
Johnson, her Havana Brown cat Everett, and a murder
that shocks coastal Oregon's beekeeping community.

Available from Kensington Publishing Corp.

Chapter 1

"Oh, Wren, what do you think?" Aunt Eloise asked as she walked into my shop, Let It Bee. She held out her Havana Brown cat, Elton, dressed in a green alien costume.

"That costume really brings out the color of his eyes," I said. My cat, Everett, meowed his agreement. Elton was Everett's uncle. My aunt had bred Havana Brown cats for years until after Everett's mother died. Then she decided that encouraging people to adopt cats was a better way to go and started a Havana Brown rescue group.

"It's for the McMinnville UFO festival," Aunt Eloise said. "You're going, right?"

I winced. "I forgot about it. But in my defense, all my time has been taken up by the Let It Bee second-anniversary celebration this weekend."

"It's only Monday, and the festival doesn't start until next Wednesday. So you have plenty of time to get ready. I'm sure Everett is looking forward to it." My only living relative and near and dear to my heart, Aunt Eloise was a tall woman with the large bones of our pioneering ancestors. At least, that's how I liked to think of it. Anyone who's played Oregon Trail, the computer game, knows it took hardy stock to make it all the way out to the Oregon coast.

Eloise had grown up in Oceanview, Oregon, along with my mother. I, myself, had spent only three years in town before going away to college. But over two years ago, I returned and started Let It Bee, a shop featuring honey and bees in a 1920s building just off Main Street and a few blocks from the beach. "I'm bringing Emma and Evangeline. You know how Everett gets jealous when his sisters get to do fun things and he's left out."

Everett meowed his thoughts on the matter. I sighed. It had been years since I'd been to the UFO festival. Based on a UFO sighting in McMinnville in the 1950s, the festival was equal parts campy, with parades and vendors selling alien souvenirs, and serious, with speakers discussing the science behind sightings.

"Fine," I said. "We'll go for the parade and shopping, but I'm not dressing up."

"Oh, goody." Aunt Eloise pulled a silver costume out of the pocket of her long cardigan sweater. "I made him this! What do you think, Everett?" She held up the metallic spacesuit.

He jumped down from the cashier counter and walked to her. Aunt Eloise bent down, and Everett sniffed the suit delicately, then meowed and rubbed up against her leg.

"He likes it!" She straightened. The smile was wide in her strong face. Her gray hair was held in a bun on top of her head, and I caught a whiff of her orange-blossom perfume. "Now we can all watch the parade in style. Wait until you see my costume. I have a necklace that looks like a collar. The cats are the owner, and I'm the pet!"

"Well, that's certainly true of all cats," I teased. "But I'm not wearing a costume."

"You said that already," she pouted a moment, then broke into a wide smile. "Is it okay if I ask Sally Hendrickson to come with us? She would wear a costume. She's into cosplay."

"Yes, that's fine," I said.

The bells on the door to the shop jangled, and my sales manager, Porsche Allen, stepped inside the door. She shook off her umbrella, folded it, and walked into the shop. "Not busy today?" She looked around the currently customer-free store.

"We had a nice rush this morning, but between the rain and school getting out soon, there's a bit of a lull," I said.

"Typical Monday," Porsche said as she put her umbrella into the holder behind the cashier stand and pulled off her raincoat. Porsche was tall and thin, with gorgeous black hair from her Korean mother and sparkling blue eyes from her American father. Today she wore jeans, black booties, and a green sweater. "Hey, Eloise, what's up?"

"We're going to the UFO festival in McMinnville this weekend," Eloise said. "Isn't Elton cute in his little green costume?" She held up her kitty and placed the silver metallic costume on the counter. "I brought this one for Everett."

At the sound of his name, Everett jumped up on the counter and brushed by Porsche so that she could stroke his brown fur.

"Nice," Porsche said. "I took the kids to that festival last year. They had a blast."

I grabbed a zippered hoody sweatshirt off the coat tree near the counter, slid it on, and then grabbed my purse. "Please tell me you didn't dress up."

"We didn't," Porsche confirmed. "But the boys want to this year."

"Oh, good, we can all go together," Aunt Eloise said.

"Well, I'll let you two figure things out. I have an appointment. Thanks for coming in a bit early and covering for me, Porsche. Is someone picking the kids up from school?"

Porsche had two boys, River and Phoenix, who were ten and eight years old, respectively. "Jason worked from home today, so he can get them." Her husband, Jason, worked for a local tech company and was able to work from home whenever he wasn't traveling.

"Great, thanks. I've got to go see a bee wrangler about the fruit-tree honey," I headed toward the door.

"Tell Elias we said hi," Aunt Eloise said.

"I will." I waved my goodbye and pulled the hood up over my curly hair to keep it from frizzing too much in the soft rain. It rained a lot in spring on the Oregon coast. Unlike Porsche and her umbrella, most natives simply put on a hooded sweatshirt and stepped out, hood up. I guess we were used to being damp.

Elias Bentwood was a bee wrangler who lived in an old house on the edge of town. He'd trained me in the art of beekeeping and was my go-to guy for local honey. If Elias didn't have it, he could point me to where to get it.

I got into my car and drove the mile or so it took to get there. The house was a one-bedroom shotgun style, which meant you could open the front door and shoot a gun straight through the house and kill someone in the back-yard. Aunt Eloise said that a bachelor lumberjack had built it in the 1920s, and it had been neglected until Elias bought it in the 1980s.

The tiny home was painted white and had sea-blue shutters. Elias maintained it well. I'd known him ever since I'd gotten out of college. Most of his hives were hired out at the moment to the farmers near Mount Hood. It was fruit-tree-blossom season, and bee wranglers would ensure there were hives close to the blossoms.

Bees typically foraged two miles from their hive, and even though some were thought to forage two to three times that distance, bee owners trucked hives in during blossom season to ensure the trees were properly polli-nated.

Elias loved his bees and wintered some of his hives behind the house. It was Elias who had helped me design the glass-walled hive that took up a portion of my shop. Bees are important to the environment, and he'd been thrilled when I told him I wanted a safe way to give my customers a look inside a working hive.

He'd helped me build the hive on the exterior of my shop and introduced the queen bee and her court to the hive. It had become so successful that it was one of the biggest draws to my shop. The kids loved to come and watch the bees work, making honeycomb and depositing honey.

The rain stopped, and the sun came out as I walked up on the porch. I pulled my hood off, letting my curls spring out, and knocked on the door. "Elias? It's Wren." There wasn't an answer, but I wasn't worried. Elias was probably out in the back with the one or two hives he hadn't hired out. I moved off the porch and followed the sidewalk around the side of the house to the back. The house didn't have a garage or even a driveway. Instead, there was a two-track alley in the back where Elias would pull his truck in and out to move the hives.

I heard someone moving through the back bushes. "Elias? It's Wren." Rounding the corner of the house, I came upon a horrifying scene. There were three hives tilted over, the roofs pushed off and the bees swarming, angry and confused. I caught the sound of car doors slamming and saw a blue car speed away down the alley.

"Elias! The bees!" Instinct had me stepping back to keep the side of the house between me and the angry bees. "Elias!" I called and peered around the house. Whoever did this must have taken off in the car. I didn't want to get stung, so I stayed on the side of the house and dialed Elias's cell phone.

I could hear ringing coming from the backyard. "Elias?" The only sound was the phone ringing, and it went quiet as I was dumped into voice mail. If Elias was in the backyard, he might be hurt or, worse, attacked by the confused bees. The only safe vantage point to find out for sure would be from inside the house. I hurried around to the front of the house.

The door was unlocked, and I walked into the small living room. "Elias? It's Wren. Are you okay?" I made my way quickly through the tidy kitchen to the bedroom in the back. No one was there. The bedroom was a mess of scattered papers and files on top of the made bed. I hurried to the back door that led out to a tiny screened porch.

Elias lay on the ground, unmoving, while the bees swarmed around him. "Elias! Don't move. I'll get help." I knew better than to rush into a swarm of angry and confused bees. I dialed 9-1-1.

"Nine-one-one. What is your emergency?"

I recognized Josie Pickler's voice. "Josie, it's Wren Johnson. I'm at Elias Bentwood's house. He's lying on the ground in his backyard and not moving. I think he's hurt."

"Okay, Wren, I've got an ambulance and police on their way. Can you check for a pulse?"

"No," I said. "Someone has disturbed Elias's bees. They're swarming the entire backyard. We'll need bee wranglers with protective gear."

"I'll call animal control," Josie said. "Or should I call an exterminator?"

"Don't call an exterminator! I don't want the bees hurt."

"I'll advise the ambulance that bees are swarming," Josie said.

"Have them park out front," I said. "I know another beekeeper. I'll hang up and call him."

"Okay," Josie said. "Stay safe."

I hung up and scrolled through my contacts to find Klaus Vanderbuen's number. Klaus was a friend of Elias, and although he lived twenty miles from town, he was the only person I could think of to call.

"Hello?" Klaus's voice was deep and comforting.

"Oh, thank goodness you answered," I said. "It's Wren Johnson. I own the bee-themed shop near Main in Oceanview. I'm a friend of Elias Bentwood."

"What's going on, Wren? You sound out of breath."

"I'm at Elias Bentwood's place. Elias is on the ground and not moving. I called emergency services, but someone has vandalized his hives. Bees are swarming everywhere. I don't think we can get to Elias to help him."

Klaus muttered something dark. "I'm on my way," he said. "Don't let anyone do anything stupid to the bees."

"I'll do my best," I said. "Please hurry. I don't know how badly Elias is hurt."

Klaus hung up the phone, and I walked back through the house to the front porch to wait for emergency services to arrive. I had some practice working with beehives, but they had always been docile. As angry as these bees were, there was no way I could reach Elias without help.

I heard sirens in the distance and ran off the porch to the street to wave them over. It was a police car. Officer Jim Hampton parked the car. Riding with him was another officer I didn't know.

"What's going on?" Jim asked when he opened his car door.

"It's Elias," I said. "He's on the ground in the back, but someone has attacked the bees, and they are too angry for me to get to Elias."

The second officer got out of the car. "I can't help," he said, his dark gaze flat. "I'm allergic to bee stings. Got an EpiPen in the glove box."

"Show me where Elias is," Jim said. He was six feet tall, had blue eyes in a tan face, and looked a bit like the actor Paul Newman. "Ashton, check out the house."

"It's open," I said. "I found the door unlocked and went inside to get a better look at the backyard."

Jim frowned at me. "Elias is in the backyard, and you went into the house?"

"Yes," I said. "It was the only way to safely see the entire backyard. It's how I found Elias." We took off down the sidewalk as I continued to explain. "I called Klaus Vanderbuen. He's the closest bee wrangler. But he's about fifteen minutes out."

Jim followed behind me. I stopped at the corner and peered around the side of the house. Jim stepped around me and then ducked back beside me. "Those are some angry bees. Any thoughts on how to handle them? Should we smoke them?"

"Smoke them?" I asked.

"You know smoke tends to calm bees."

"I think that only works if you are gently moving parts of the hive," I said. "You need protective gear and maybe a bee box to capture them."

"I'll call it in," he grabbed his radio. As he spoke into it, I crouched down, wondering if I could somehow crawl slowly toward Elias. But the bees swarmed the entire backyard.

"Ashton," I heard Jim say into the radio when I moved back beside him.

"Yeah, boss," the radio crackled.

"Can you see anything from inside the house?" Jim asked.

"I'm looking out the bedroom window. Bees are swarming the back porch as well as the yard. Looks like we have one man down and three hives demolished. I don't see how whoever did this got away without being stung multiple times."

"I'll put a call into the ER to watch for bee attacks," Jim said. "Can you tell if Elias is moving?"

"I'm not seeing any motion," Officer Ashton said. "Looks like maybe blood pooling near his head. Also the back bedroom looks tossed."

"I can hear the ambulance," I said and hurried back to the front of the house. The ambulance arrived, and I rushed to the driver's side. EMT Sarah Ritter stepped out. She was five foot nine with short brown hair and serious eyes.

"What do we have?" she asked as she headed to the back of her rig to get out her equipment.

"Bees," I said. "Are you allergic?"

"Nope," she replied and opened the back door. I saw Jim go into the house as the second EMT came around and parked behind the ambulance.

It was Rick Fender. He was my height, and rail thin with bleached blond hair and a surfer look. He grinned at me. "Maybe you can lure them out with that honey candy you make."

"There are three hives of angry bees," I said. "I don't think my candy is going to soothe them. I hope you're not allergic."

"I'm not," he said and grabbed the end of a stretcher.

"Where's the victim?" Ritter asked.

"He's in the backyard, but the bees are there, too, and they're swarming. Listen, I called a bee wrangler." I glanced at my phone. "He should be here in about ten minutes."

"The victim could be dead by then," Ritter said and pulled the stretcher and her kit toward the side of the house.

"I don't think you understand," I said. "The bees are bad."

"I'm not afraid of a few stings," Ritter said and moved quickly down the side of the house.

"Fine," I said and threw up my hands. "Don't say I didn't warn you."

They rounded the back of the house, and I counted to myself. "Five, four, three—" Both EMTs came scrambling back to the side of the building without the stretcher.

Ritter waved a bee from in front of her face and stopped next to me. "That's more than a few angry bees. You run the honey shop. Do you have a bee suit?"

"No, I only wrangled for a season and used one of Elias's suits," I said.

"How far out is the bee wrangler?" Jim asked as he and Officer Ashton stepped off the porch.

I glanced at my phone, "Maybe ten minutes? Is there anything we can do in the meantime? Elias could be dying."

"I hate to break it to you," Jim said. "But until we get those bees under control, there's no getting to Elias."

"I can try a hazmat suit," Sarah said. "We have a couple back at the station. Don't know if they will be protective enough against that many bees. But it's worth a try."

"Go get it," Jim said. "Ashton and I will stay here and monitor the situation."

"Dispatch wanted to call animal control," I said. "But even if they have a bee suit, Klaus will get here before they can dig it out."

"What if Elias moves?" Jim asked. "Will the bees attack him?"

"There's a chance they will," I said.

"Then we'd better hope he keeps his head down," Jim said. "Fender, monitor the victim from a safe distance. Ritter, go get the hazmat suit."

"And me?" I asked.

"Stay out of the way."

Connect with U(s)

Visit us online at
KensingtonBooks.com
to read more from your favorite authors, see books
by series, view reading group guides, and more.

Join us on social media

for sneak peeks, chances to win books and prize packs,
and to share your thoughts with other readers.

facebook.com/kensingtonpublishing
twitter.com/kensingtonbooks

Tell us what you think!

To share your thoughts, submit a review,
or sign up for our eNewsletters, please visit:
KensingtonBooks.com/TellUs.